Aetheric Mechanics
A Graphic Novella

story
WARREN ELLIS

pencils
GIANLUCA PAGLIARANI

inks
CHRIS DREIER

convention cover color
JUANMAR

editor-in-chief
WILLIAM CHRISTENSEN

creative director
MARK SEIFERT

chief mechanic
ARIANA OSBORNE

marketing director
DAVID MARKS

D1377652

www.avatarpress.com

AETHERIC MECHANICS. Sept 2008.
Published by Avatar Press, Inc.,
515 N. Century Blvd. Rantoul, IL 61866.
©2008 Avatar Press, Inc.

Aetheric Mechanics and all related
properties TM & ©2008 Warren Ellis.

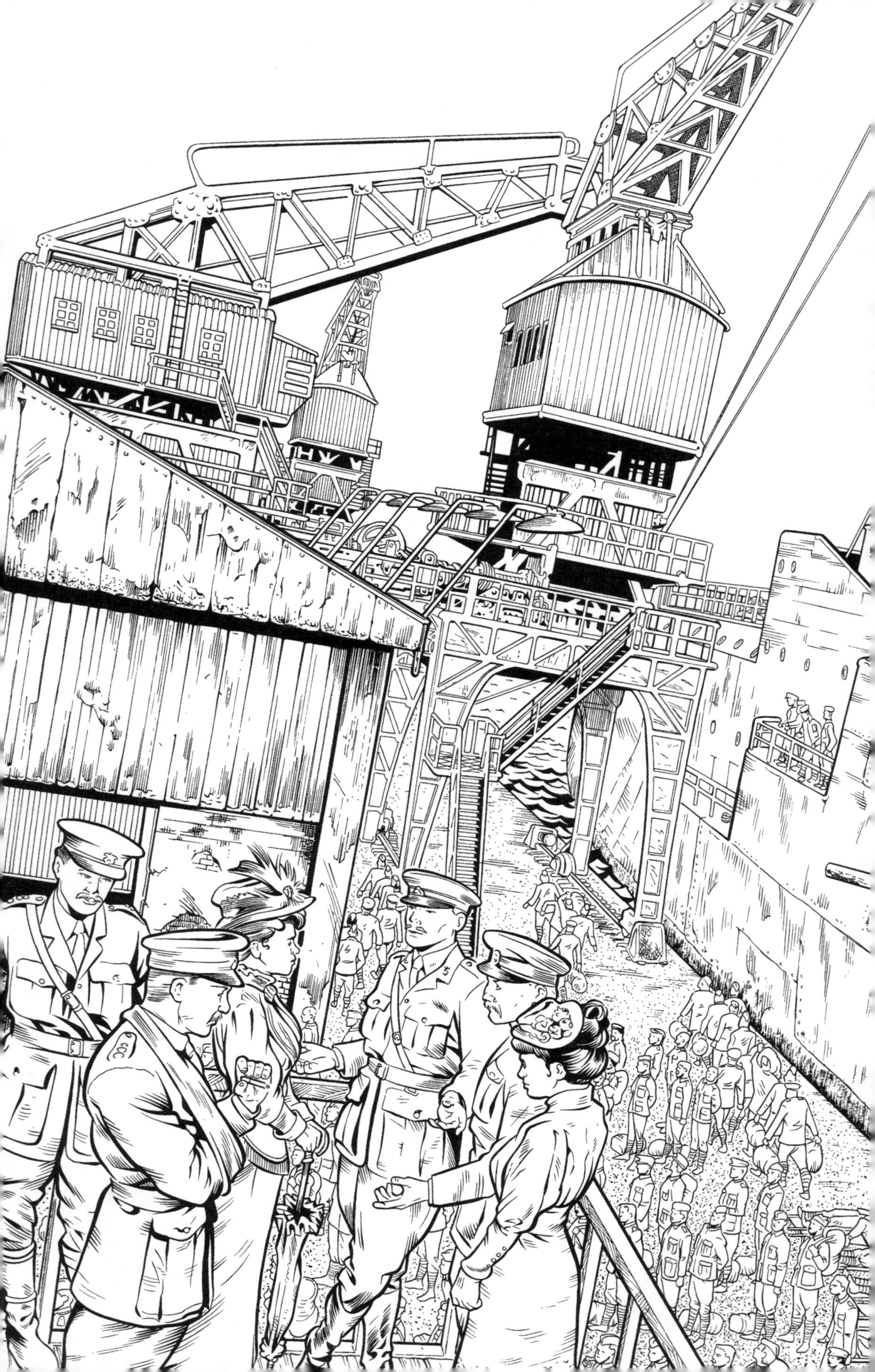

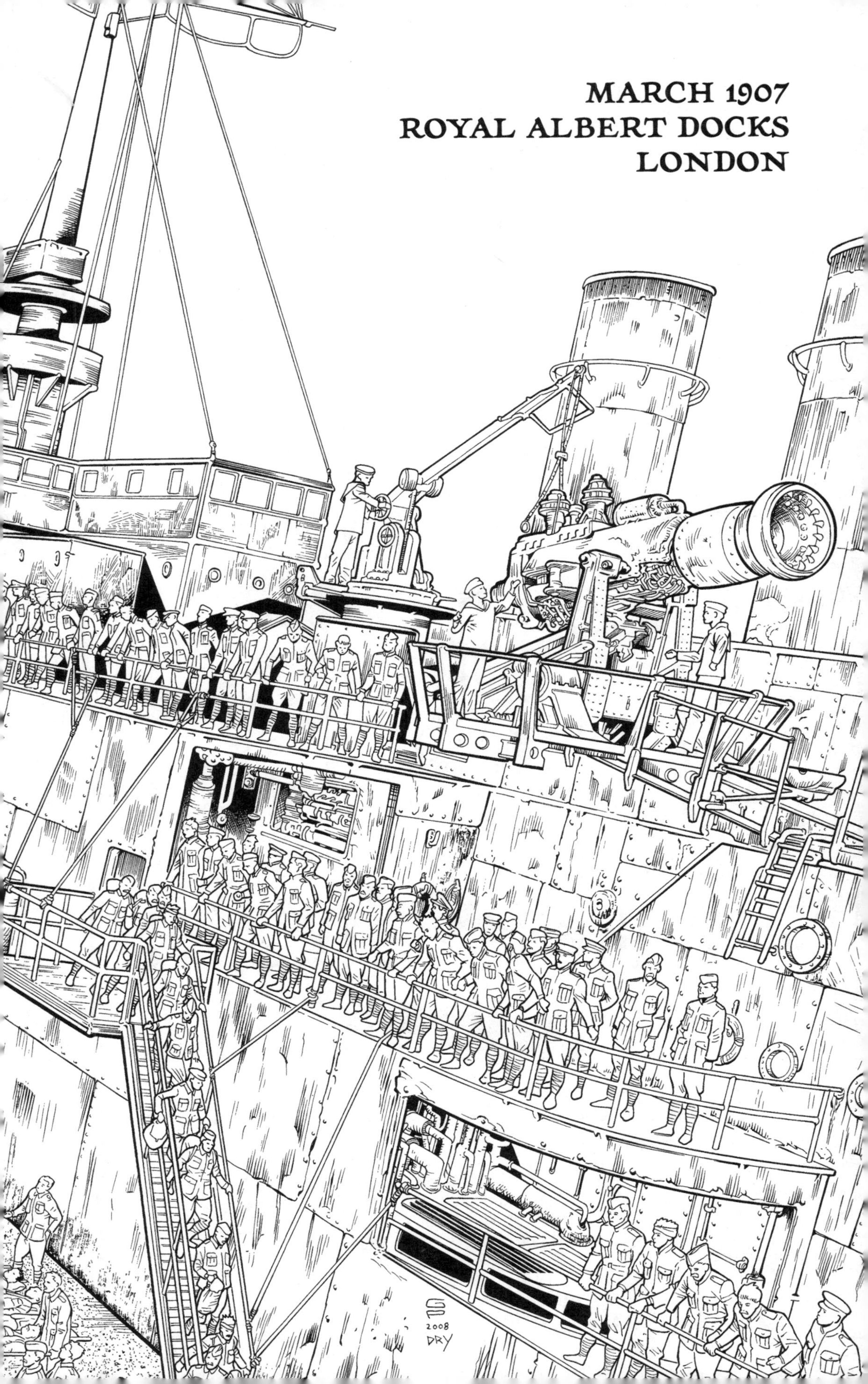
MARCH 1907
ROYAL ALBERT DOCKS
LONDON
2008
DRY

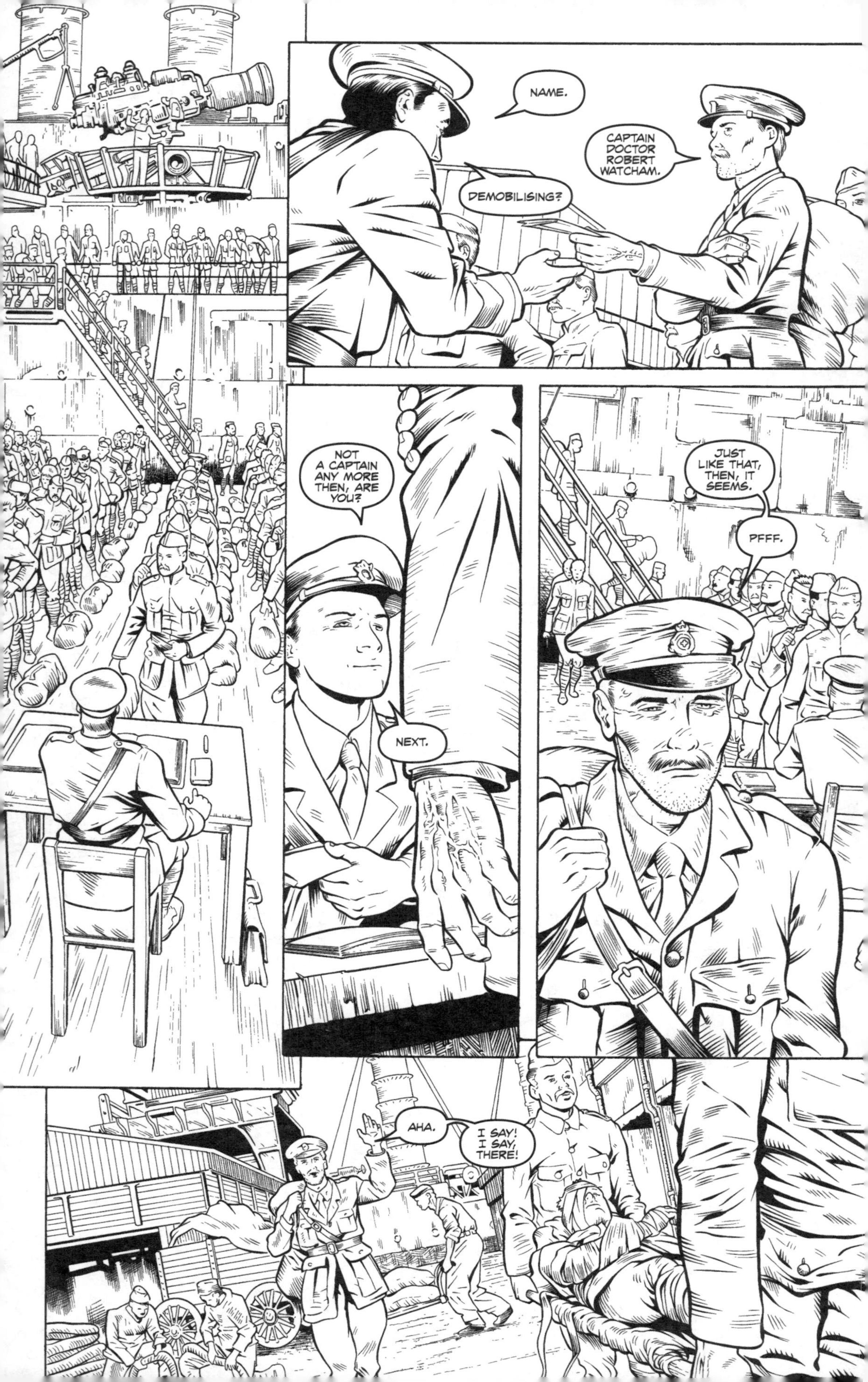
NAME.
CAPTAIN DOCTOR ROBERT WATCHAM.
DEMOBILISING?
NOT A CAPTAIN ANY MORE THEN, ARE YOU?
NEXT.
JUST LIKE THAT, THEN, IT SEEMS.
PFFF.
AHA.
I SAY! I SAY, THERE!

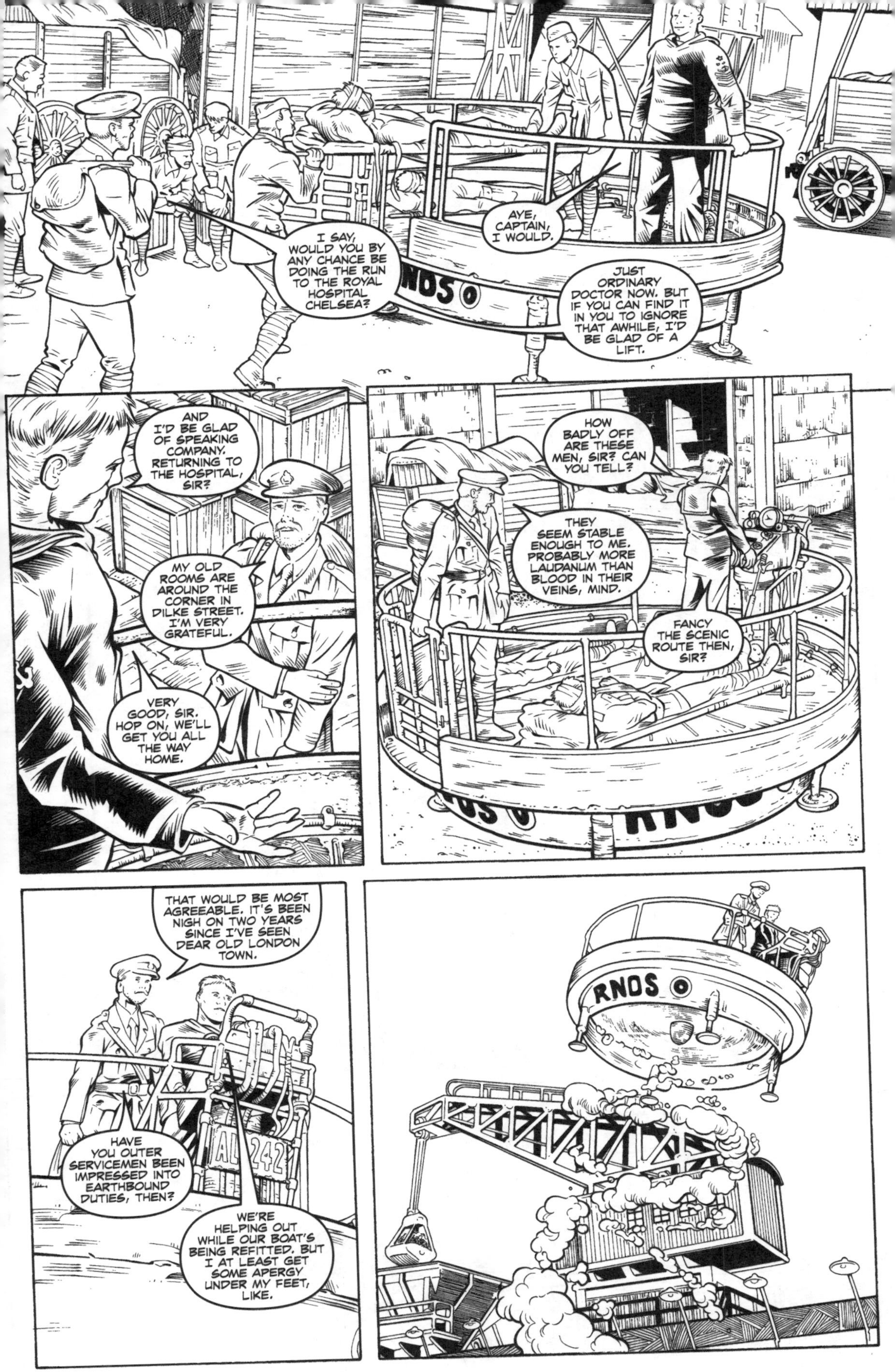

I SAY, WOULD YOU BY ANY CHANCE BE DOING THE RUN TO THE ROYAL HOSPITAL CHELSEA?
AYE, CAPTAIN, I WOULD.
JUST ORDINARY DOCTOR NOW. BUT IF YOU CAN FIND IT IN YOU TO IGNORE THAT AWHILE, I'D BE GLAD OF A LIFT.
RNOS
AND I'D BE GLAD OF SPEAKING COMPANY. RETURNING TO THE HOSPITAL, SIR?
MY OLD ROOMS ARE AROUND THE CORNER IN DILKE STREET. I'M VERY GRATEFUL.
VERY GOOD, SIR. HOP ON, WE'LL GET YOU ALL THE WAY HOME.
HOW BADLY OFF ARE THESE MEN, SIR? CAN YOU TELL?
THEY SEEM STABLE ENOUGH TO ME. PROBABLY MORE LAUDANUM THAN BLOOD IN THEIR VEINS, MIND.
FANCY THE SCENIC ROUTE THEN, SIR?
THAT WOULD BE MOST AGREEABLE. IT'S BEEN NIGH ON TWO YEARS SINCE I'VE SEEN DEAR OLD LONDON TOWN.
HAVE YOU OUTER SERVICEMEN BEEN IMPRESSED INTO EARTHBOUND DUTIES, THEN?
WE'RE HELPING OUT WHILE OUR BOAT'S BEING REFITTED. BUT I AT LEAST GET SOME APERGY UNDER MY FEET, LIKE.
AL 242
RNOS

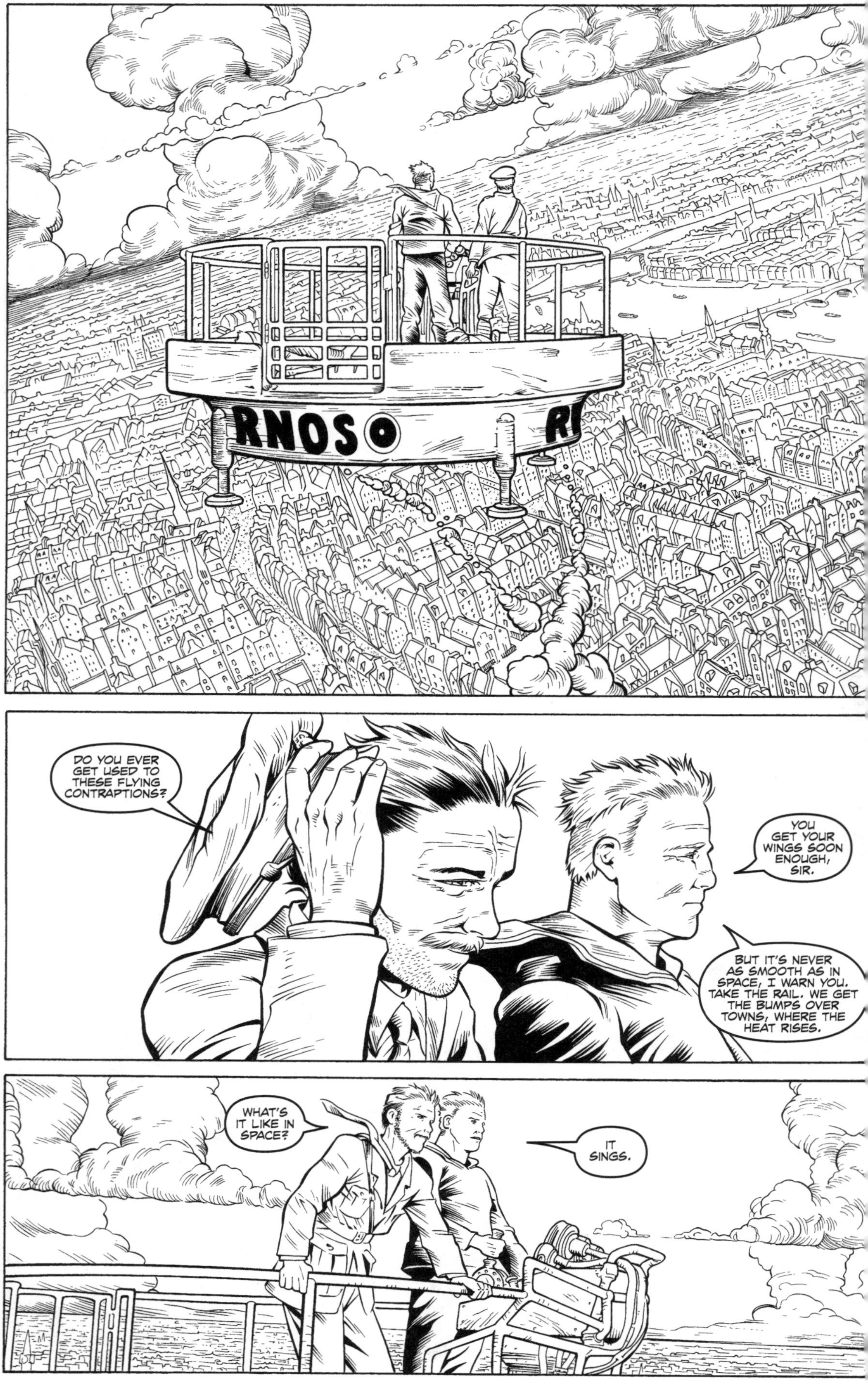
RNOS
DO YOU EVER GET USED TO THESE FLYING CONTRAPTIONS?
YOU GET YOUR WINGS SOON ENOUGH, SIR.
BUT IT'S NEVER AS SMOOTH AS IN SPACE, I WARN YOU. TAKE THE RAIL. WE GET THE BUMPS OVER TOWNS, WHERE THE HEAT RISES.
WHAT'S IT LIKE IN SPACE?
IT SINGS.

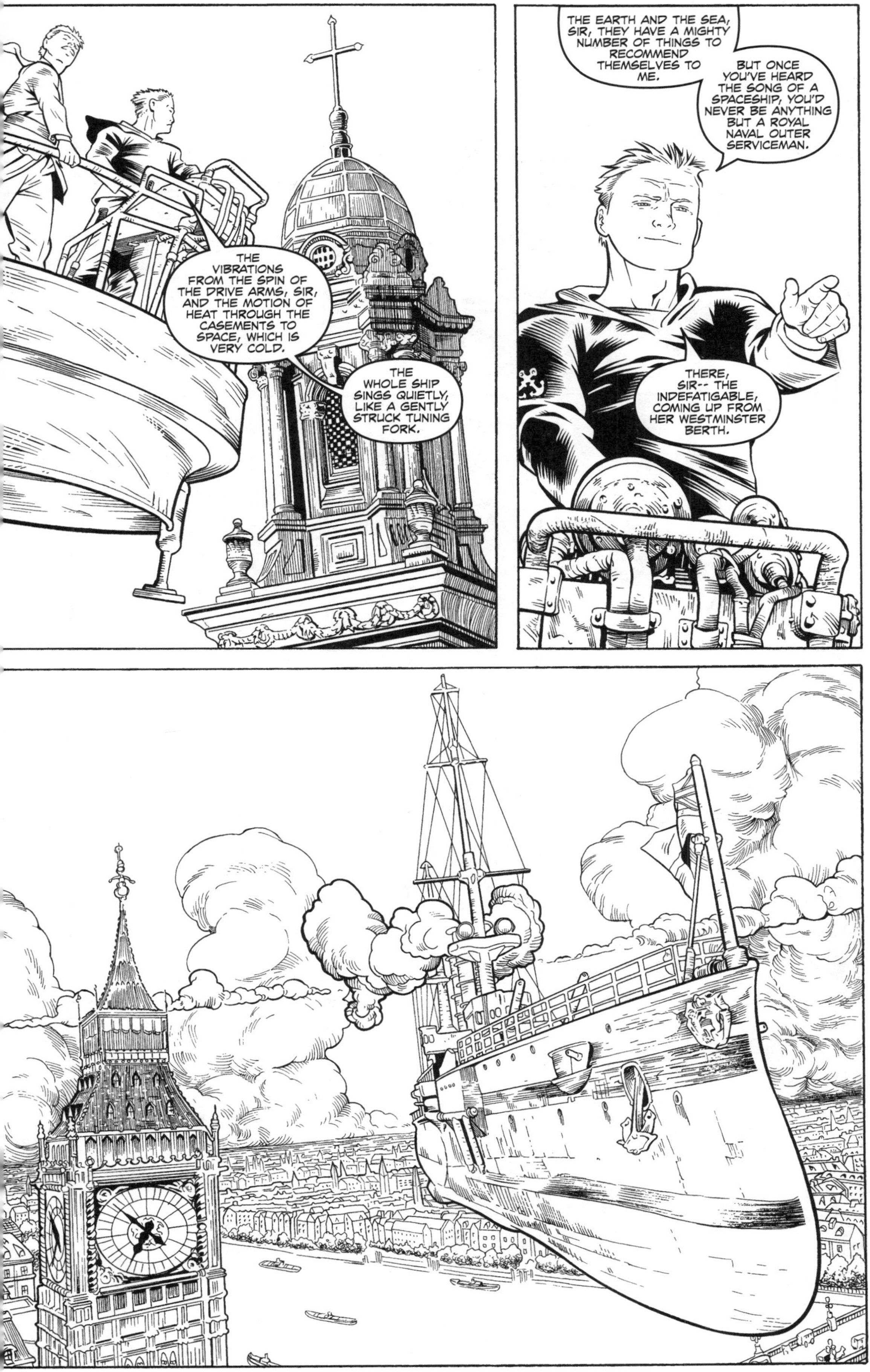
THE VIBRATIONS FROM THE SPIN OF THE DRIVE ARMS, SIR, AND THE MOTION OF HEAT THROUGH THE CASEMENTS TO SPACE, WHICH IS VERY COLD.
THE WHOLE SHIP SINGS QUIETLY, LIKE A GENTLY STRUCK TUNING FORK.
THE EARTH AND THE SEA, SIR, THEY HAVE A MIGHTY NUMBER OF THINGS TO RECOMMEND THEMSELVES TO ME.
BUT ONCE YOU'VE HEARD THE SONG OF A SPACESHIP, YOU'D NEVER BE ANYTHING BUT A ROYAL NAVAL OUTER SERVICEMAN.
THERE, SIR-- THE INDEFATIGABLE, COMING UP FROM HER WESTMINSTER BERTH.

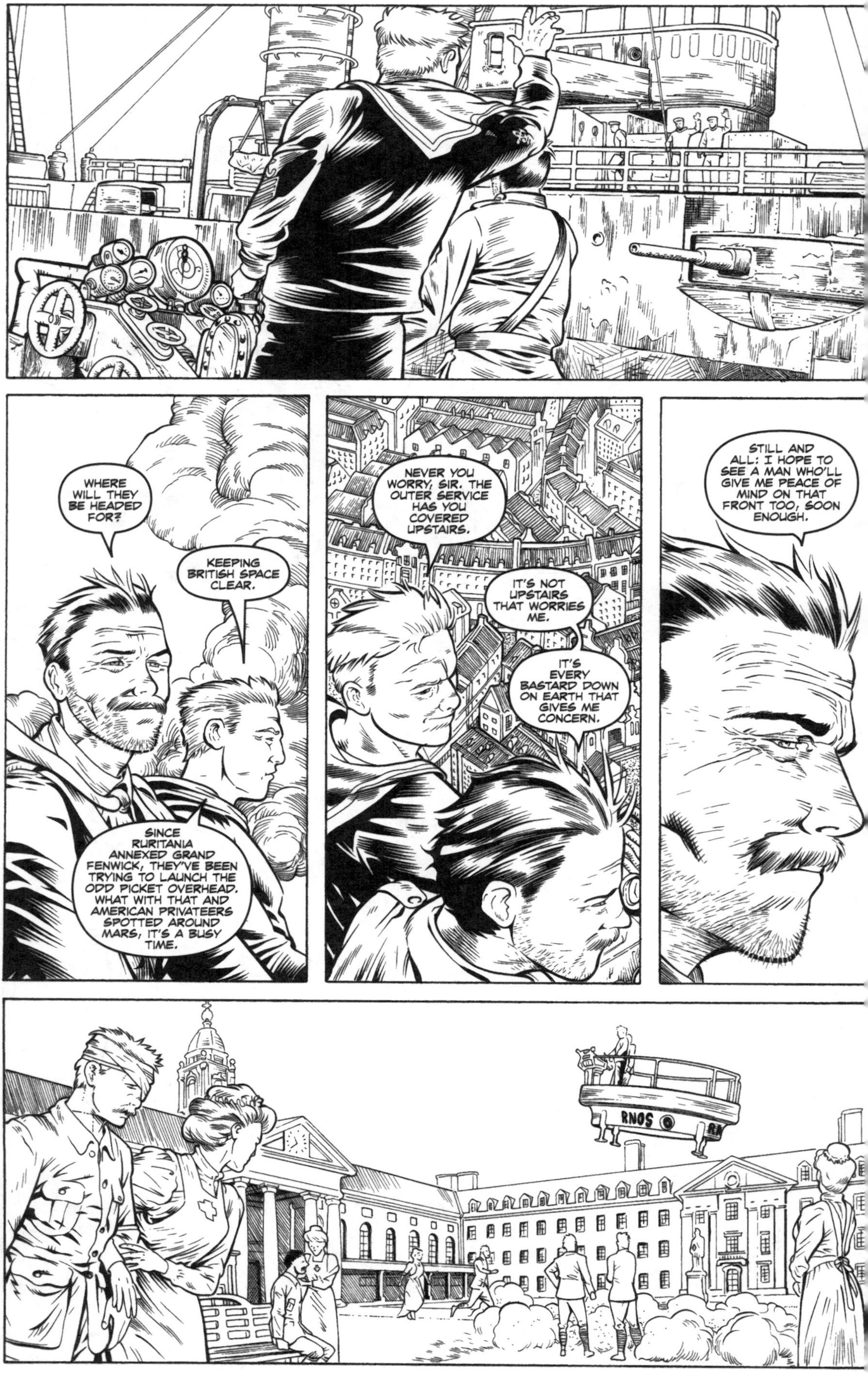
WHERE WILL THEY BE HEADED FOR?
KEEPING BRITISH SPACE CLEAR.
SINCE RURITANIA ANNEXED GRAND FENWICK, THEY'VE BEEN TRYING TO LAUNCH THE ODD PICKET OVERHEAD. WHAT WITH THAT AND AMERICAN PRIVATEERS SPOTTED AROUND MARS, IT'S A BUSY TIME.
NEVER YOU WORRY, SIR. THE OUTER SERVICE HAS YOU COVERED UPSTAIRS.
IT'S NOT UPSTAIRS THAT WORRIES ME.
IT'S EVERY BASTARD DOWN ON EARTH THAT GIVES ME CONCERN.
STILL AND ALL: I HOPE TO SEE A MAN WHO'LL GIVE ME PEACE OF MIND ON THAT FRONT TOO, SOON ENOUGH.
RNOS

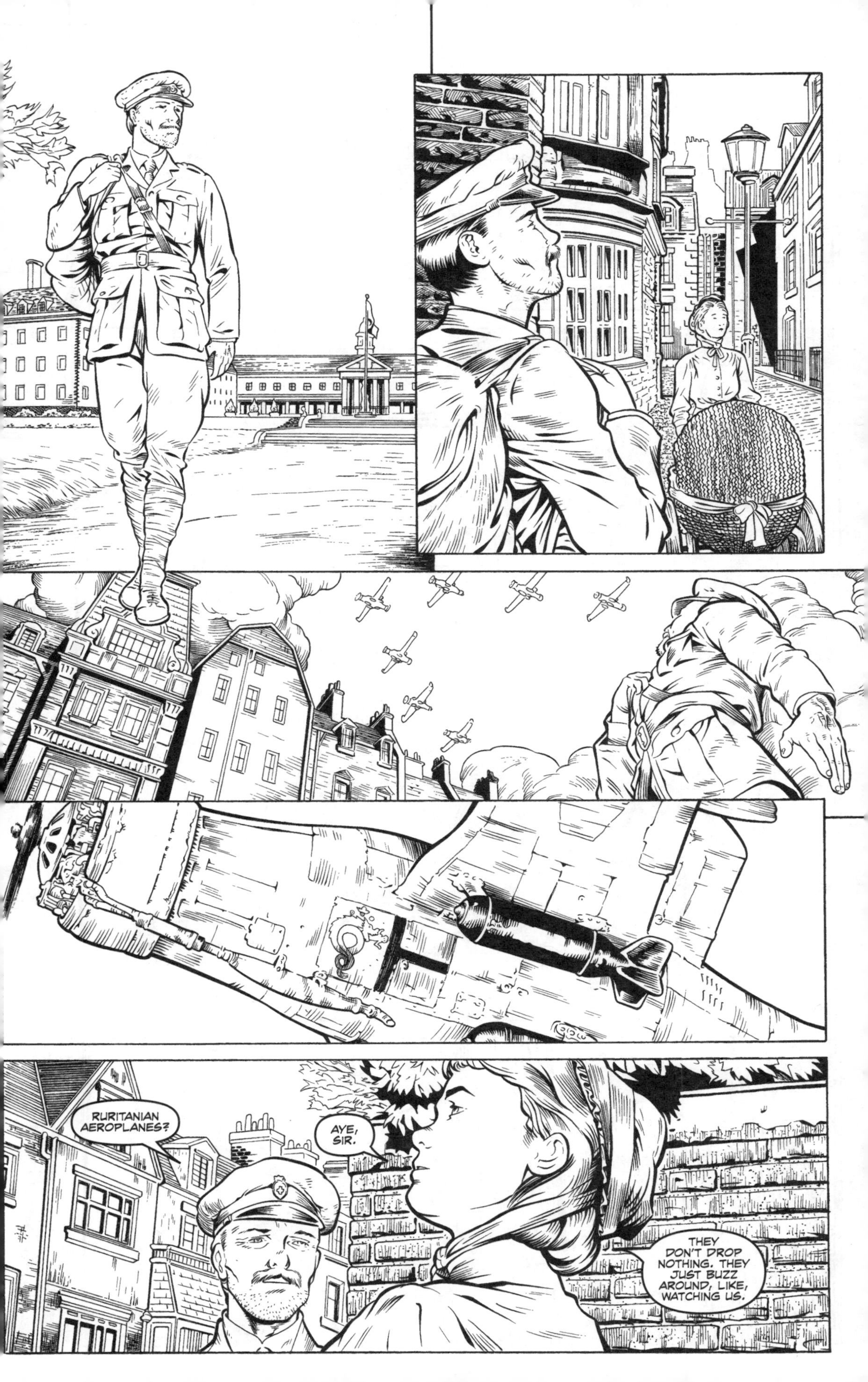
RURITANIAN AEROPLANES?
AYE, SIR.
THEY DON'T DROP NOTHING. THEY JUST BUZZ AROUND, LIKE, WATCHING US.

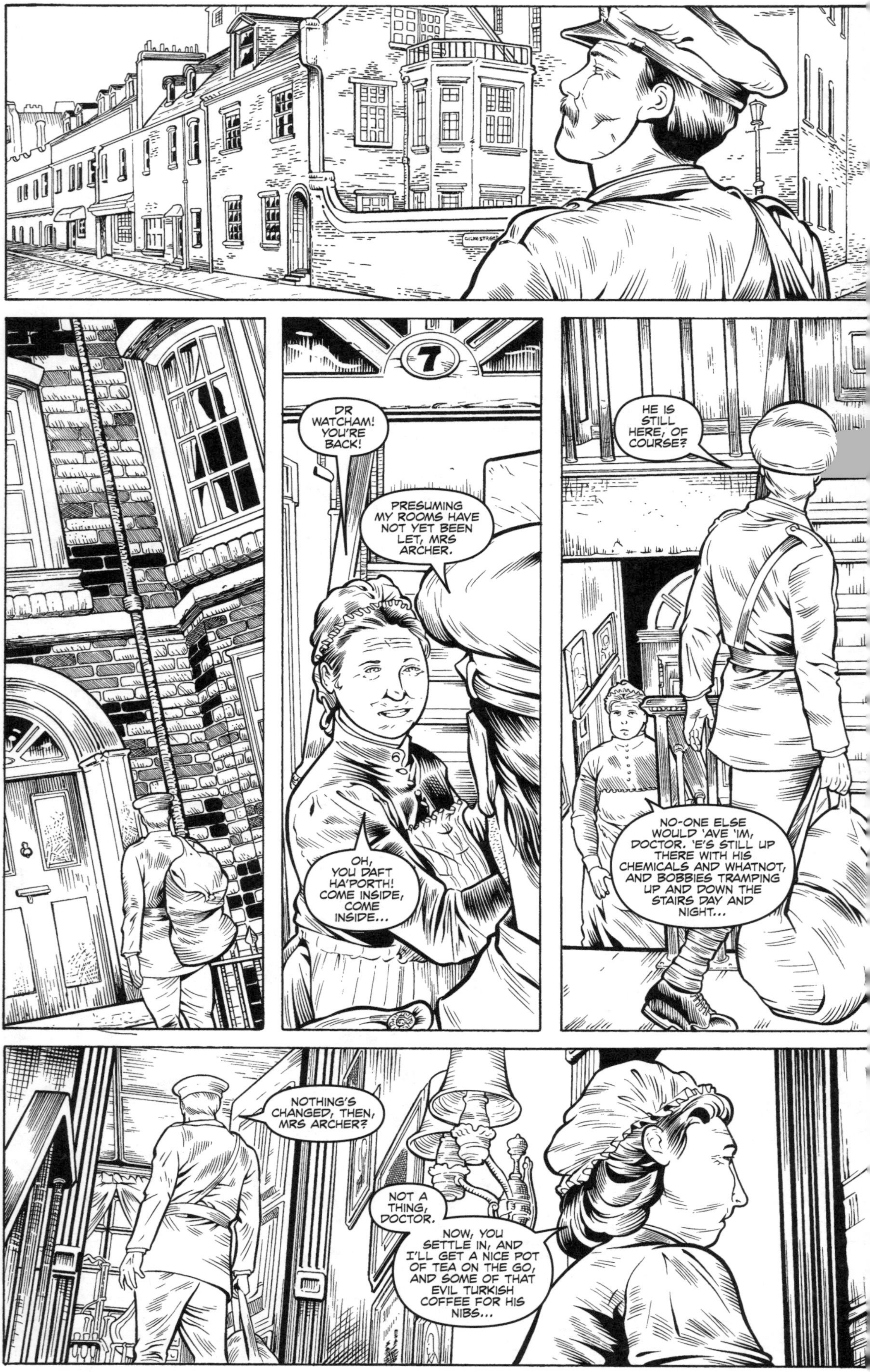
DR WATCHAM! YOU'RE BACK!
PRESUMING MY ROOMS HAVE NOT YET BEEN LET, MRS ARCHER.
OH, YOU DAFT HA'PORTH! COME INSIDE, COME INSIDE...
HE IS STILL HERE, OF COURSE?
NO-ONE ELSE WOULD 'AVE 'IM, DOCTOR. 'E'S STILL UP THERE WITH HIS CHEMICALS AND WHATNOT, AND BOBBIES TRAMPING UP AND DOWN THE STAIRS DAY AND NIGHT...
NOTHING'S CHANGED, THEN, MRS ARCHER?
NOT A THING, DOCTOR.
NOW, YOU SETTLE IN, AND I'LL GET A NICE POT OF TEA ON THE GO, AND SOME OF THAT EVIL TURKISH COFFEE FOR HIS NIBS...

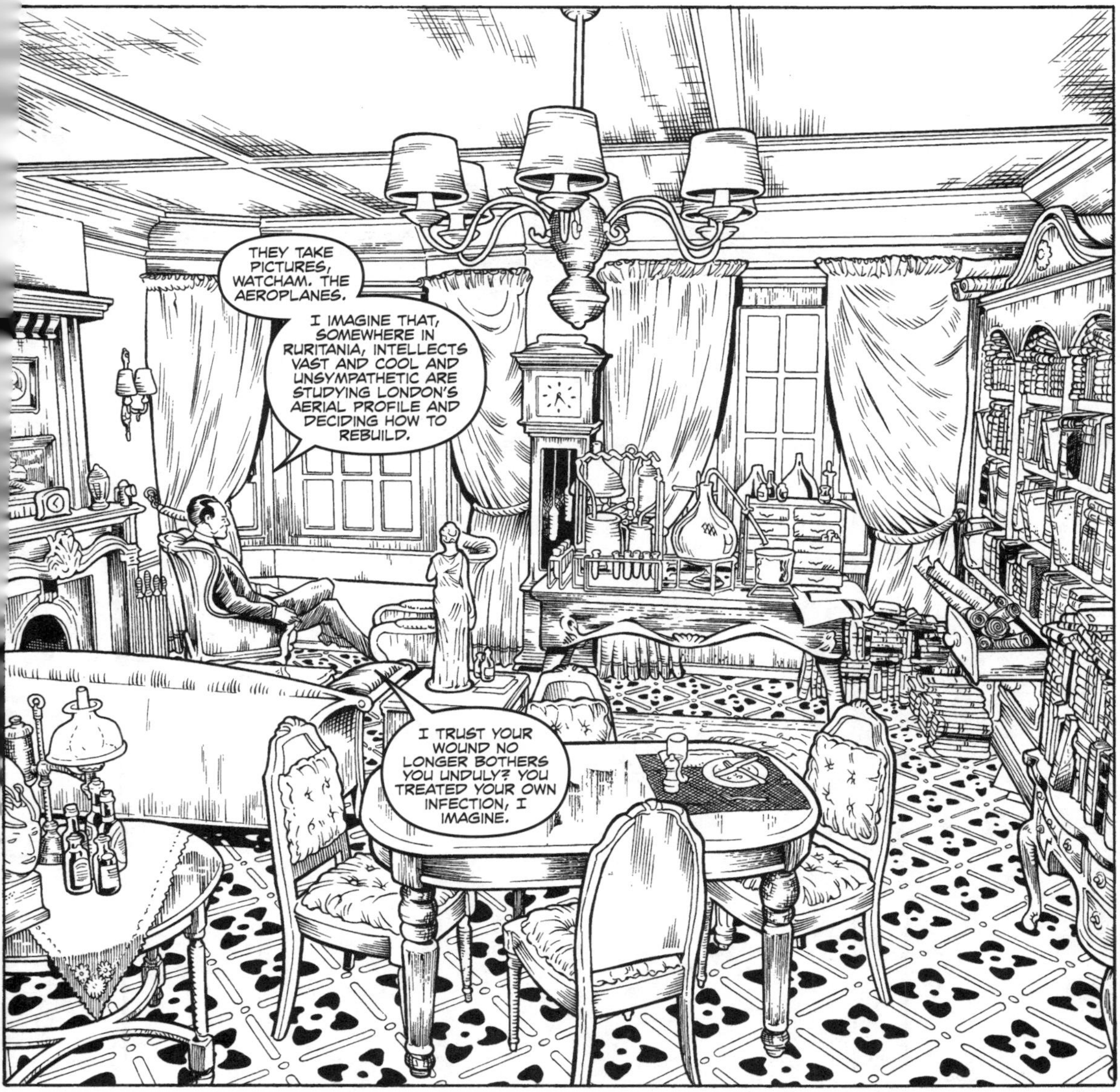
THEY TAKE PICTURES, WATCHAM. THE AEROPLANES.
I IMAGINE THAT, SOMEWHERE IN RURITANIA, INTELLECTS VAST AND COOL AND UNSYMPATHETIC ARE STUDYING LONDON'S AERIAL PROFILE AND DECIDING HOW TO REBUILD.
I TRUST YOUR WOUND NO LONGER BOTHERS YOU UNDULY? YOU TREATED YOUR OWN INFECTION, I IMAGINE.

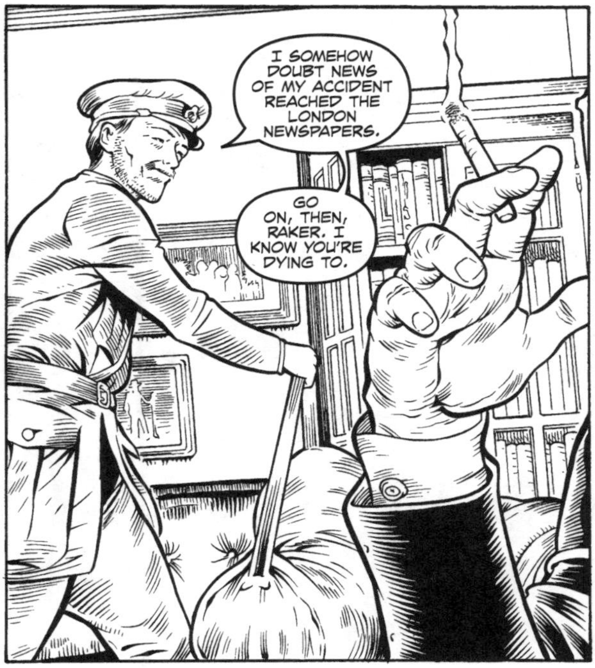
I SOMEHOW DOUBT NEWS OF MY ACCIDENT REACHED THE LONDON NEWSPAPERS.
GO ON, THEN, RAKER. I KNOW YOU'RE DYING TO.

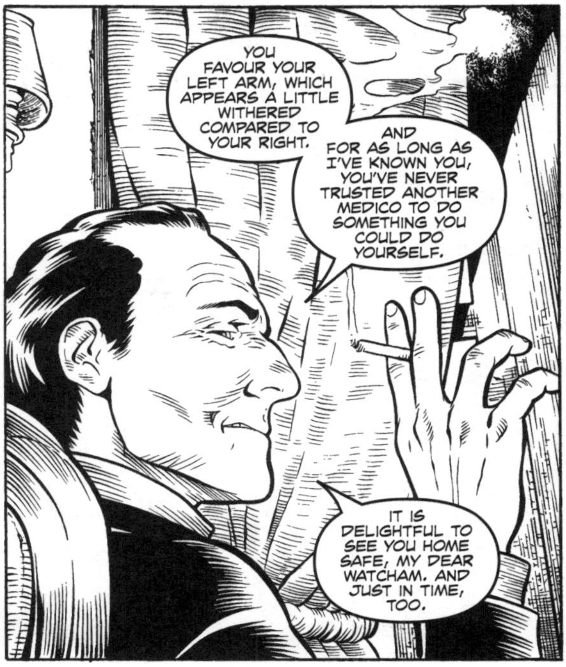
YOU FAVOUR YOUR LEFT ARM, WHICH APPEARS A LITTLE WITHERED COMPARED TO YOUR RIGHT.
AND FOR AS LONG AS I'VE KNOWN YOU, YOU'VE NEVER TRUSTED ANOTHER MEDICO TO DO SOMETHING YOU COULD DO YOURSELF.
IT IS DELIGHTFUL TO SEE YOU HOME SAFE, MY DEAR WATCHAM. AND JUST IN TIME, TOO.

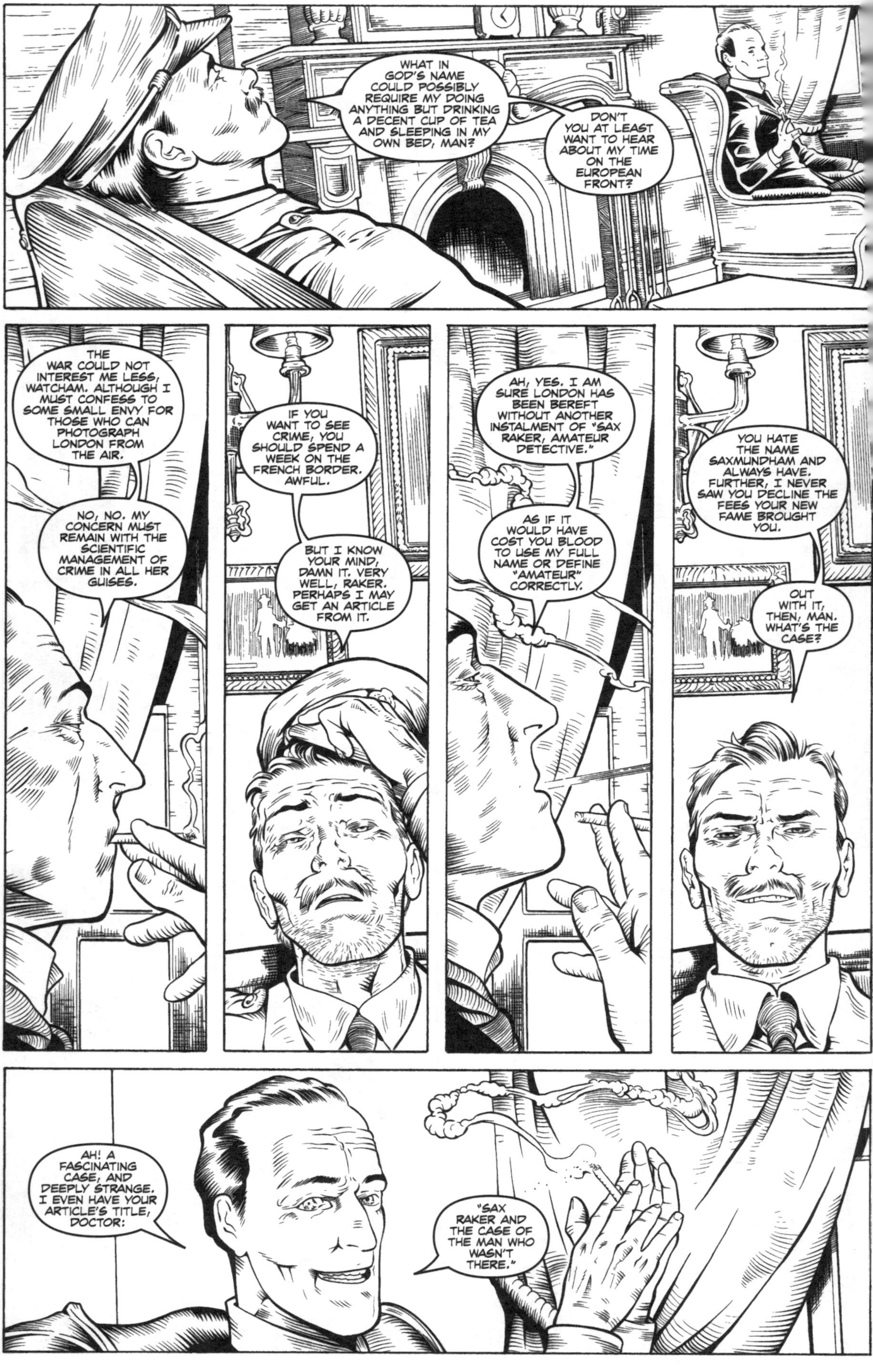
WHAT IN GOD'S NAME COULD POSSIBLY REQUIRE MY DOING ANYTHING BUT DRINKING A DECENT CUP OF TEA AND SLEEPING IN MY OWN BED, MAN?
DON'T YOU AT LEAST WANT TO HEAR ABOUT MY TIME ON THE EUROPEAN FRONT?
THE WAR COULD NOT INTEREST ME LESS, WATCHAM. ALTHOUGH I MUST CONFESS TO SOME SMALL ENVY FOR THOSE WHO CAN PHOTOGRAPH LONDON FROM THE AIR.
NO, NO. MY CONCERN MUST REMAIN WITH THE SCIENTIFIC MANAGEMENT OF CRIME IN ALL HER GUISES.
IF YOU WANT TO SEE CRIME, YOU SHOULD SPEND A WEEK ON THE FRENCH BORDER. AWFUL.
BUT I KNOW YOUR MIND, DAMN IT. VERY WELL, RAKER. PERHAPS I MAY GET AN ARTICLE FROM IT.
AH, YES. I AM SURE LONDON HAS BEEN BEREFT WITHOUT ANOTHER INSTALMENT OF "SAX RAKER, AMATEUR DETECTIVE."
AS IF IT WOULD HAVE COST YOU BLOOD TO USE MY FULL NAME OR DEFINE "AMATEUR" CORRECTLY.
YOU HATE THE NAME SAXMUNDHAM AND ALWAYS HAVE. FURTHER, I NEVER SAW YOU DECLINE THE FEES YOUR NEW FAME BROUGHT YOU.
OUT WITH IT, THEN, MAN. WHAT'S THE CASE?
AH! A FASCINATING CASE, AND DEEPLY STRANGE. I EVEN HAVE YOUR ARTICLE'S TITLE, DOCTOR:
"SAX RAKER AND THE CASE OF THE MAN WHO WASN'T THERE."

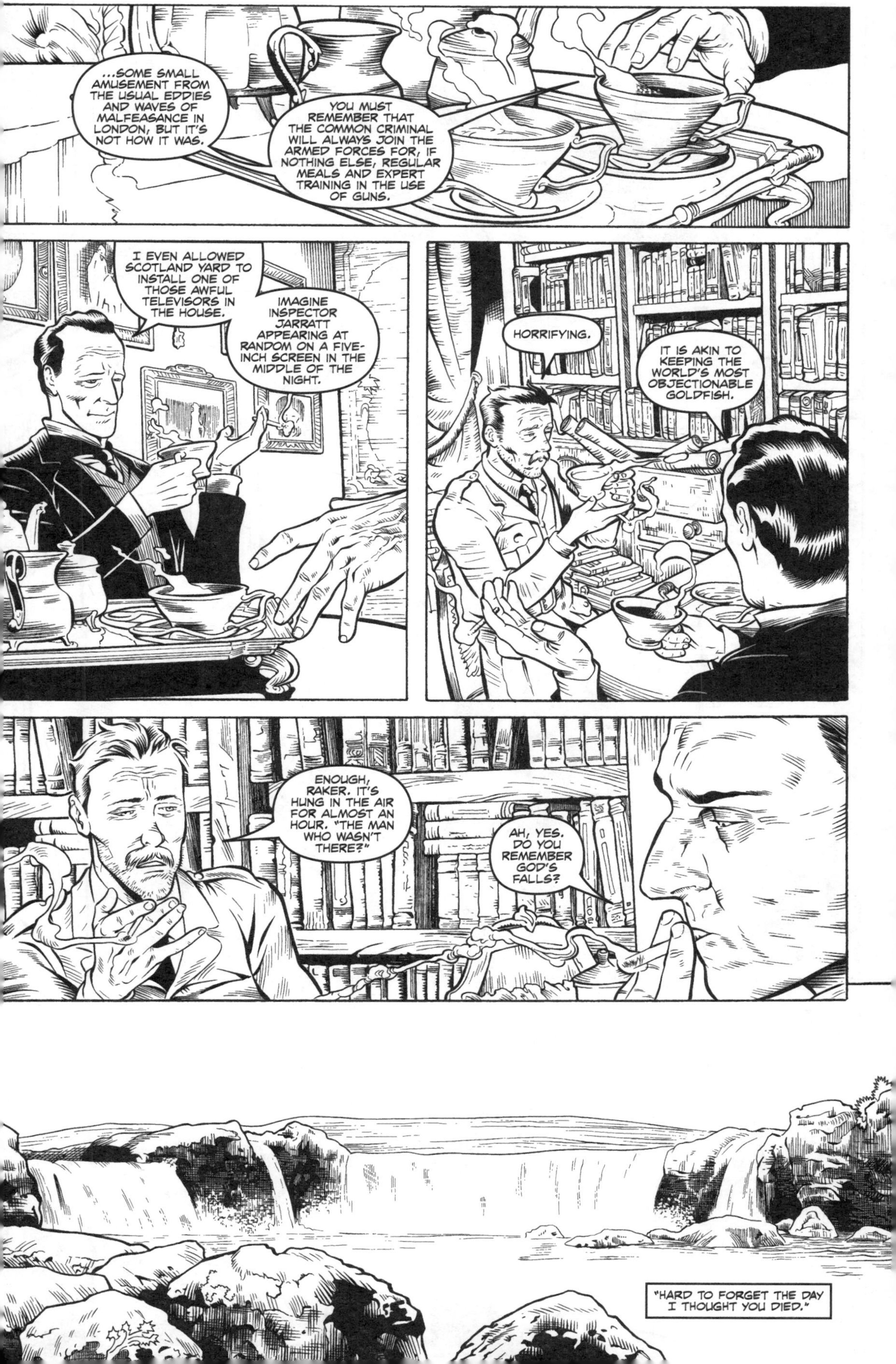
...SOME SMALL AMUSEMENT FROM THE USUAL EDDIES AND WAVES OF MALFEASANCE IN LONDON, BUT IT'S NOT HOW IT WAS.
YOU MUST REMEMBER THAT THE COMMON CRIMINAL WILL ALWAYS JOIN THE ARMED FORCES FOR, IF NOTHING ELSE, REGULAR MEALS AND EXPERT TRAINING IN THE USE OF GUNS.
I EVEN ALLOWED SCOTLAND YARD TO INSTALL ONE OF THOSE AWFUL TELEVISORS IN THE HOUSE.
IMAGINE INSPECTOR JARRATT APPEARING AT RANDOM ON A FIVE-INCH SCREEN IN THE MIDDLE OF THE NIGHT.
HORRIFYING.
IT IS AKIN TO KEEPING THE WORLD'S MOST OBJECTIONABLE GOLDFISH.
ENOUGH, RAKER. IT'S HUNG IN THE AIR FOR ALMOST AN HOUR. "THE MAN WHO WASN'T THERE?"
AH, YES. DO YOU REMEMBER GOD'S FALLS?
"HARD TO FORGET THE DAY I THOUGHT YOU DIED."

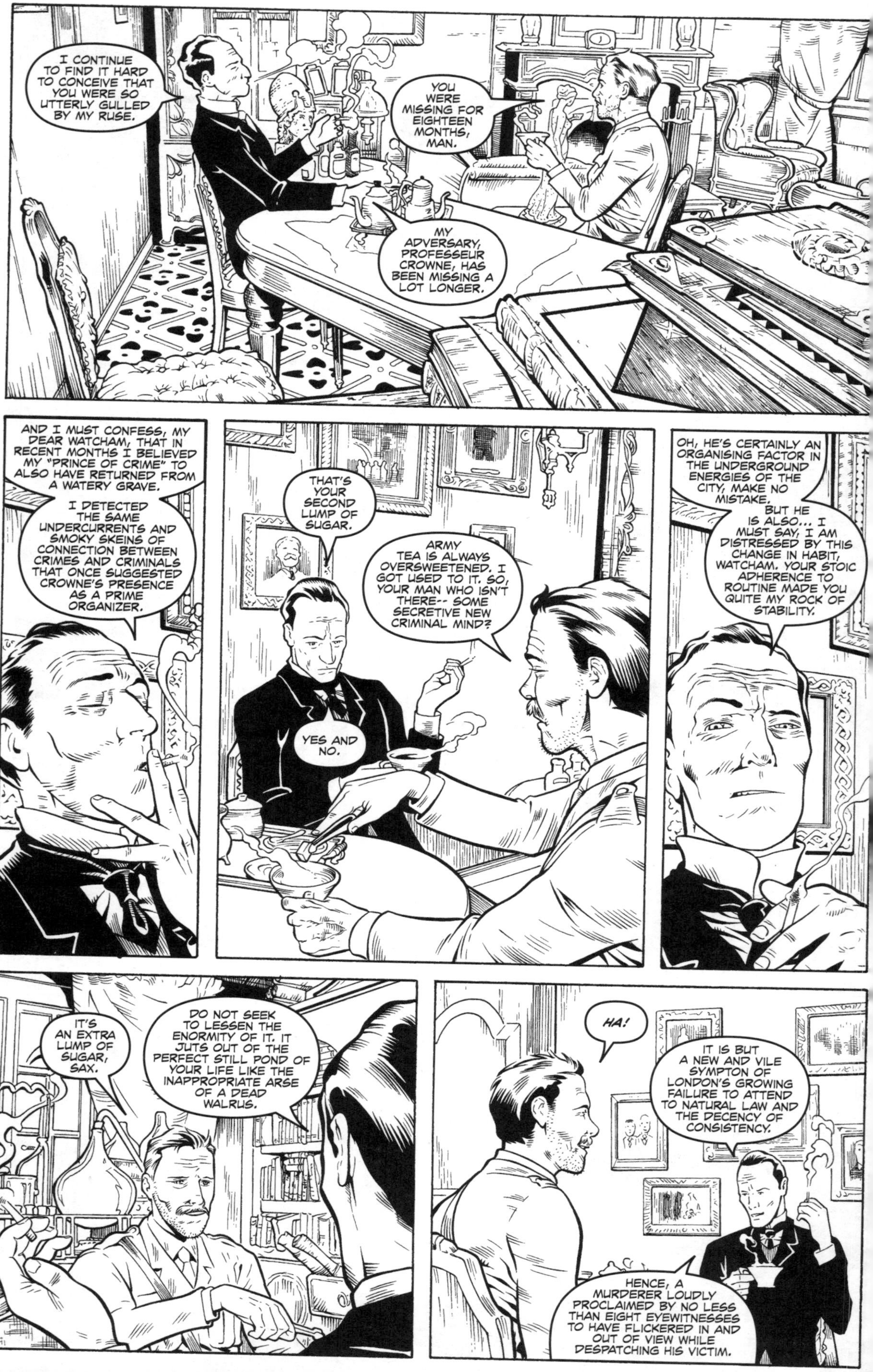
I CONTINUE TO FIND IT HARD TO CONCEIVE THAT YOU WERE SO UTTERLY GULLED BY MY RUSE.
YOU WERE MISSING FOR EIGHTEEN MONTHS, MAN.
MY ADVERSARY, PROFESSEUR CROWNE, HAS BEEN MISSING A LOT LONGER.
AND I MUST CONFESS, MY DEAR WATCHAM, THAT IN RECENT MONTHS I BELIEVED MY "PRINCE OF CRIME" TO ALSO HAVE RETURNED FROM A WATERY GRAVE.
I DETECTED THE SAME UNDERCURRENTS AND SMOKY SKEINS OF CONNECTION BETWEEN CRIMES AND CRIMINALS THAT ONCE SUGGESTED CROWNE'S PRESENCE AS A PRIME ORGANIZER.
THAT'S YOUR SECOND LUMP OF SUGAR.
ARMY TEA IS ALWAYS OVERSWEETENED. I GOT USED TO IT. SO, YOUR MAN WHO ISN'T THERE-- SOME SECRETIVE NEW CRIMINAL MIND?
YES AND NO.
OH, HE'S CERTAINLY AN ORGANISING FACTOR IN THE UNDERGROUND ENERGIES OF THE CITY, MAKE NO MISTAKE.
BUT HE IS ALSO... I MUST SAY, I AM DISTRESSED BY THIS CHANGE IN HABIT, WATCHAM. YOUR STOIC ADHERENCE TO ROUTINE MADE YOU QUITE MY ROCK OF STABILITY.
IT'S AN EXTRA LUMP OF SUGAR, SAX.
DO NOT SEEK TO LESSEN THE ENORMITY OF IT. IT JUTS OUT OF THE PERFECT STILL POND OF YOUR LIFE LIKE THE INAPPROPRIATE ARSE OF A DEAD WALRUS.
HA!
IT IS BUT A NEW AND VILE SYMPTON OF LONDON'S GROWING FAILURE TO ATTEND TO NATURAL LAW AND THE DECENCY OF CONSISTENCY.
HENCE, A MURDERER LOUDLY PROCLAIMED BY NO LESS THAN EIGHT EYEWITNESSES TO HAVE FLICKERED IN AND OUT OF VIEW WHILE DESPATCHING HIS VICTIM.

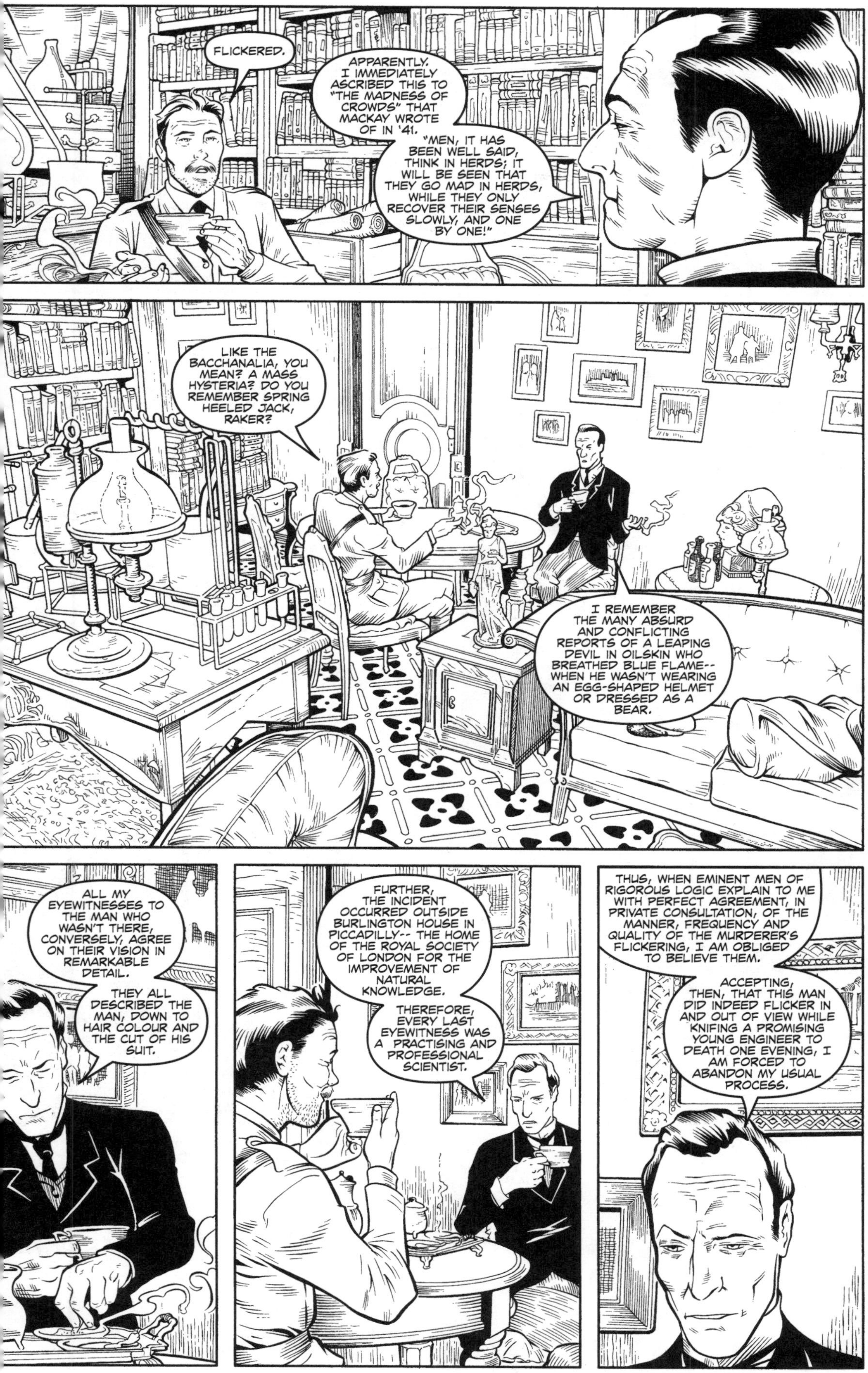
FLICKERED.
APPARENTLY. I IMMEDIATELY ASCRIBED THIS TO "THE MADNESS OF CROWDS" THAT MACKAY WROTE OF IN '41.
"MEN, IT HAS BEEN WELL SAID, THINK IN HERDS; IT WILL BE SEEN THAT THEY GO MAD IN HERDS, WHILE THEY ONLY RECOVER THEIR SENSES SLOWLY, AND ONE BY ONE!"
LIKE THE BACCHANALIA, YOU MEAN? A MASS HYSTERIA? DO YOU REMEMBER SPRING HEELED JACK, RAKER?
I REMEMBER THE MANY ABSURD AND CONFLICTING REPORTS OF A LEAPING DEVIL IN OILSKIN WHO BREATHED BLUE FLAME-- WHEN HE WASN'T WEARING AN EGG-SHAPED HELMET OR DRESSED AS A BEAR.
ALL MY EYEWITNESSES TO THE MAN WHO WASN'T THERE, CONVERSELY, AGREE ON THEIR VISION IN REMARKABLE DETAIL.
THEY ALL DESCRIBED THE MAN, DOWN TO HAIR COLOUR AND THE CUT OF HIS SUIT.
FURTHER, THE INCIDENT OCCURRED OUTSIDE BURLINGTON HOUSE IN PICCADILLY-- THE HOME OF THE ROYAL SOCIETY OF LONDON FOR THE IMPROVEMENT OF NATURAL KNOWLEDGE.
THEREFORE, EVERY LAST EYEWITNESS WAS A PRACTISING AND PROFESSIONAL SCIENTIST.
THUS, WHEN EMINENT MEN OF RIGOROUS LOGIC EXPLAIN TO ME WITH PERFECT AGREEMENT, IN PRIVATE CONSULTATION, OF THE MANNER, FREQUENCY AND QUALITY OF THE MURDERER'S FLICKERING, I AM OBLIGED TO BELIEVE THEM.
ACCEPTING, THEN, THAT THIS MAN DID INDEED FLICKER IN AND OUT OF VIEW WHILE KNIFING A PROMISING YOUNG ENGINEER TO DEATH ONE EVENING, I AM FORCED TO ABANDON MY USUAL PROCESS.

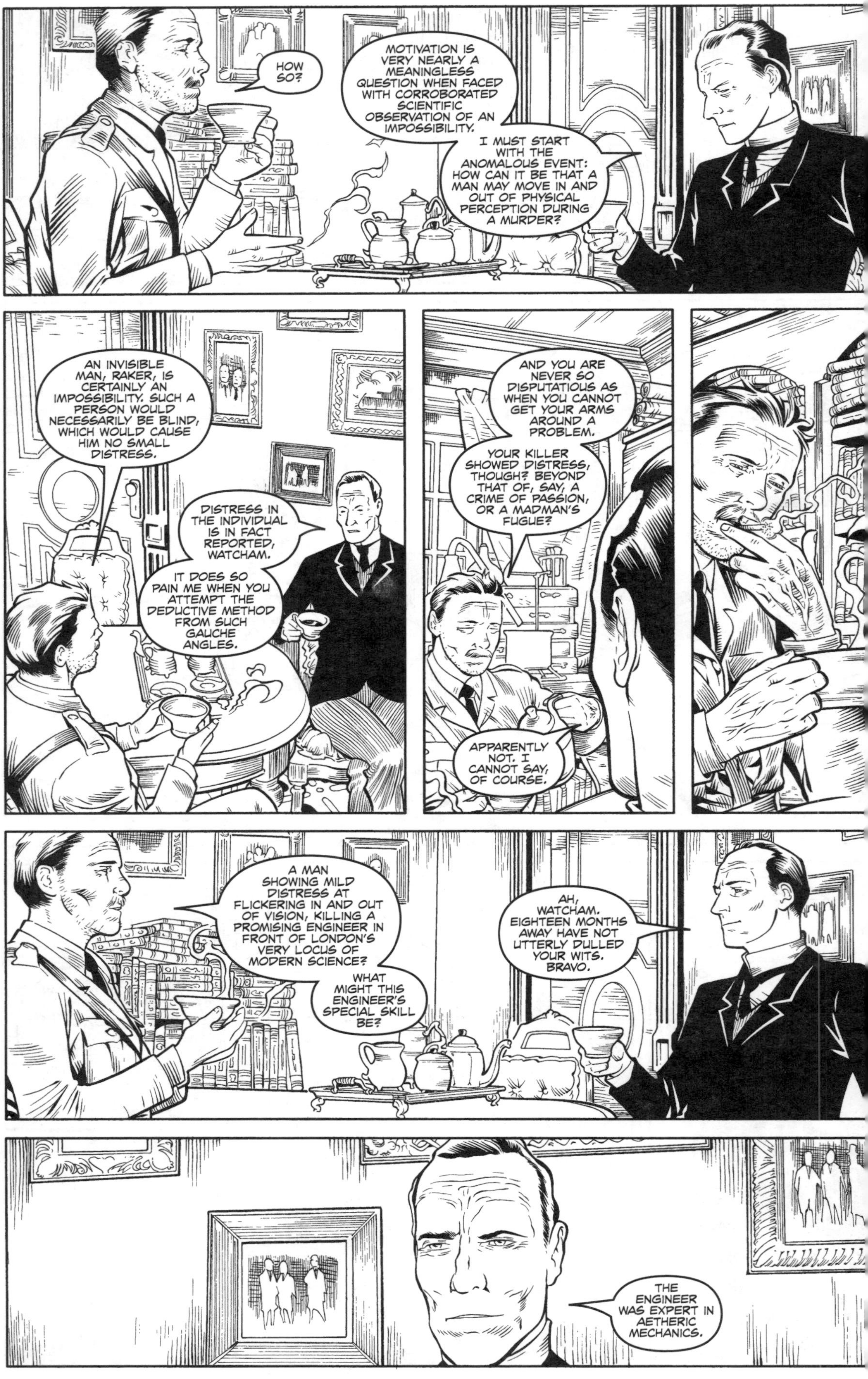
HOW SO?
MOTIVATION IS VERY NEARLY A MEANINGLESS QUESTION WHEN FACED WITH CORROBORATED SCIENTIFIC OBSERVATION OF AN IMPOSSIBILITY.
I MUST START WITH THE ANOMALOUS EVENT: HOW CAN IT BE THAT A MAN MAY MOVE IN AND OUT OF PHYSICAL PERCEPTION DURING A MURDER?
AN INVISIBLE MAN, RAKER, IS CERTAINLY AN IMPOSSIBILITY. SUCH A PERSON WOULD NECESSARILY BE BLIND, WHICH WOULD CAUSE HIM NO SMALL DISTRESS.
DISTRESS IN THE INDIVIDUAL IS IN FACT REPORTED, WATCHAM.
IT DOES SO PAIN ME WHEN YOU ATTEMPT THE DEDUCTIVE METHOD FROM SUCH GAUCHE ANGLES.
AND YOU ARE NEVER SO DISPUTATIOUS AS WHEN YOU CANNOT GET YOUR ARMS AROUND A PROBLEM.
YOUR KILLER SHOWED DISTRESS, THOUGH? BEYOND THAT OF, SAY, A CRIME OF PASSION, OR A MADMAN'S FUGUE?
APPARENTLY NOT. I CANNOT SAY, OF COURSE.
A MAN SHOWING MILD DISTRESS AT FLICKERING IN AND OUT OF VISION, KILLING A PROMISING ENGINEER IN FRONT OF LONDON'S VERY LOCUS OF MODERN SCIENCE?
WHAT MIGHT THIS ENGINEER'S SPECIAL SKILL BE?
AH, WATCHAM. EIGHTEEN MONTHS AWAY HAVE NOT UTTERLY DULLED YOUR WITS. BRAVO.
THE ENGINEER WAS EXPERT IN AETHERIC MECHANICS.

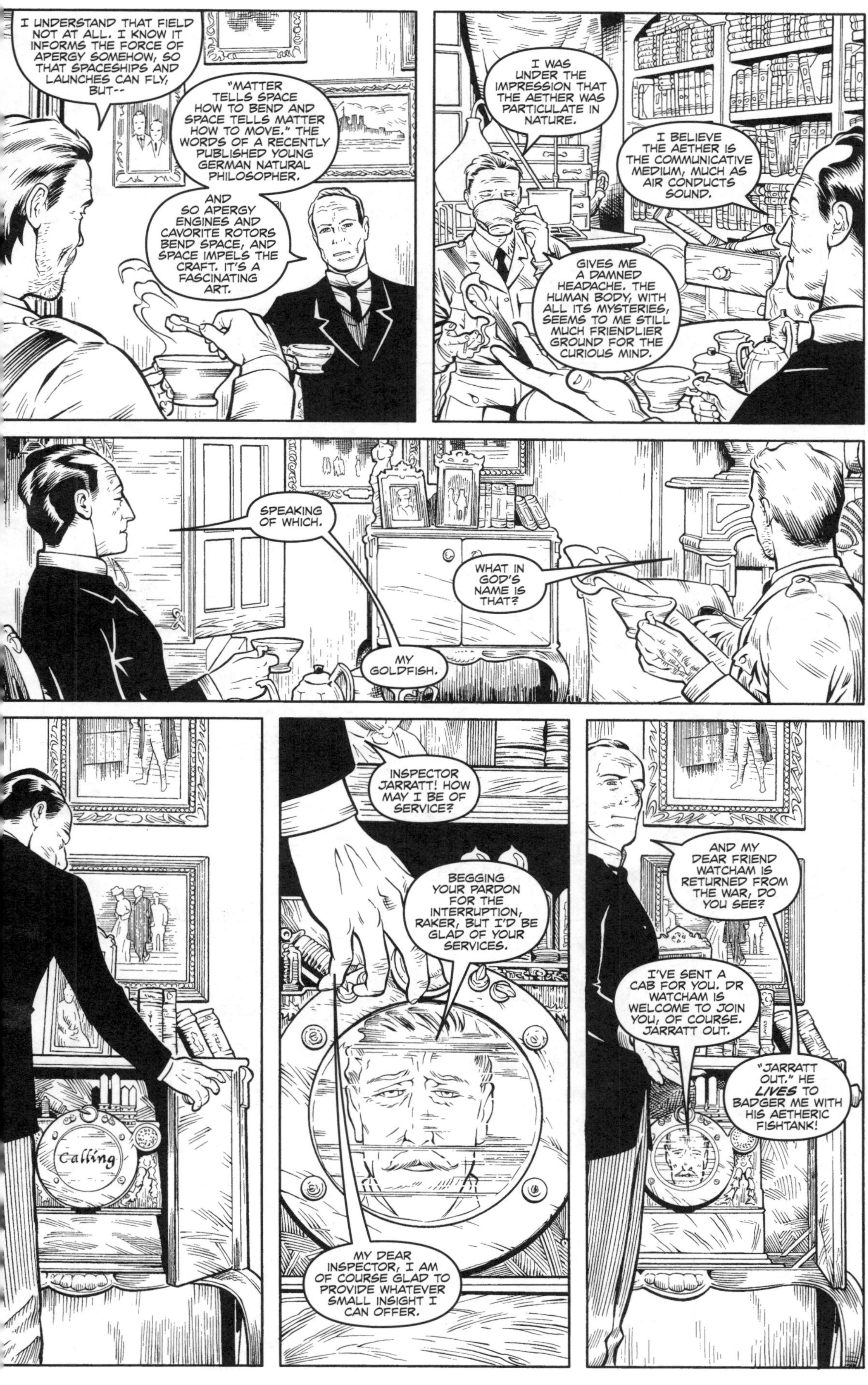
I UNDERSTAND THAT FIELD NOT AT ALL. I KNOW IT INFORMS THE FORCE OF APERGY SOMEHOW, SO THAT SPACESHIPS AND LAUNCHES CAN FLY, BUT--
"MATTER TELLS SPACE HOW TO BEND AND SPACE TELLS MATTER HOW TO MOVE." THE WORDS OF A RECENTLY PUBLISHED YOUNG GERMAN NATURAL PHILOSOPHER.
AND SO APERGY ENGINES AND CAVORITE ROTORS BEND SPACE, AND SPACE IMPELS THE CRAFT. IT'S A FASCINATING ART.
I WAS UNDER THE IMPRESSION THAT THE AETHER WAS PARTICULATE IN NATURE.
I BELIEVE THE AETHER IS THE COMMUNICATIVE MEDIUM, MUCH AS AIR CONDUCTS SOUND.
GIVES ME A DAMNED HEADACHE. THE HUMAN BODY, WITH ALL ITS MYSTERIES, SEEMS TO ME STILL MUCH FRIENDLIER GROUND FOR THE CURIOUS MIND.
SPEAKING OF WHICH.
WHAT IN GOD'S NAME IS THAT?
MY GOLDFISH.
Calling
INSPECTOR JARRATT! HOW MAY I BE OF SERVICE?
BEGGING YOUR PARDON FOR THE INTERRUPTION, RAKER, BUT I'D BE GLAD OF YOUR SERVICES.
MY DEAR INSPECTOR, I AM OF COURSE GLAD TO PROVIDE WHATEVER SMALL INSIGHT I CAN OFFER.
AND MY DEAR FRIEND WATCHAM IS RETURNED FROM THE WAR, DO YOU SEE?
I'VE SENT A CAB FOR YOU. DR WATCHAM IS WELCOME TO JOIN YOU, OF COURSE. JARRATT OUT.
"JARRATT OUT." HE LIVES TO BADGER ME WITH HIS AETHERIC FISHTANK!

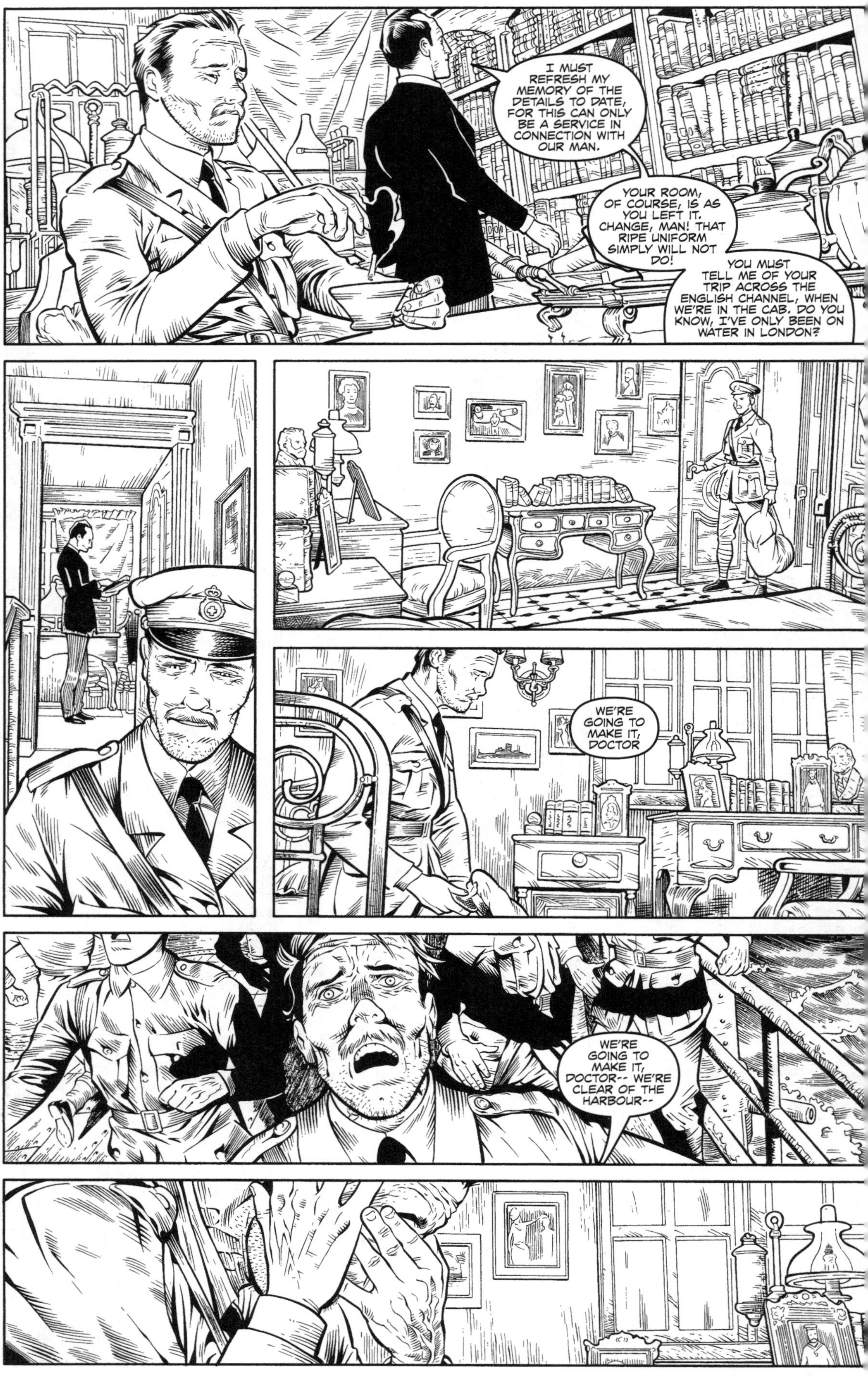
I MUST REFRESH MY MEMORY OF THE DETAILS TO DATE, FOR THIS CAN ONLY BE A SERVICE IN CONNECTION WITH OUR MAN.
YOUR ROOM, OF COURSE, IS AS YOU LEFT IT. CHANGE, MAN! THAT RIPE UNIFORM SIMPLY WILL NOT DO!
YOU MUST TELL ME OF YOUR TRIP ACROSS THE ENGLISH CHANNEL, WHEN WE'RE IN THE CAB. DO YOU KNOW, I'VE ONLY BEEN ON WATER IN LONDON?
WE'RE GOING TO MAKE IT, DOCTOR
WE'RE GOING TO MAKE IT, DOCTOR-- WE'RE CLEAR OF THE HARBOUR--

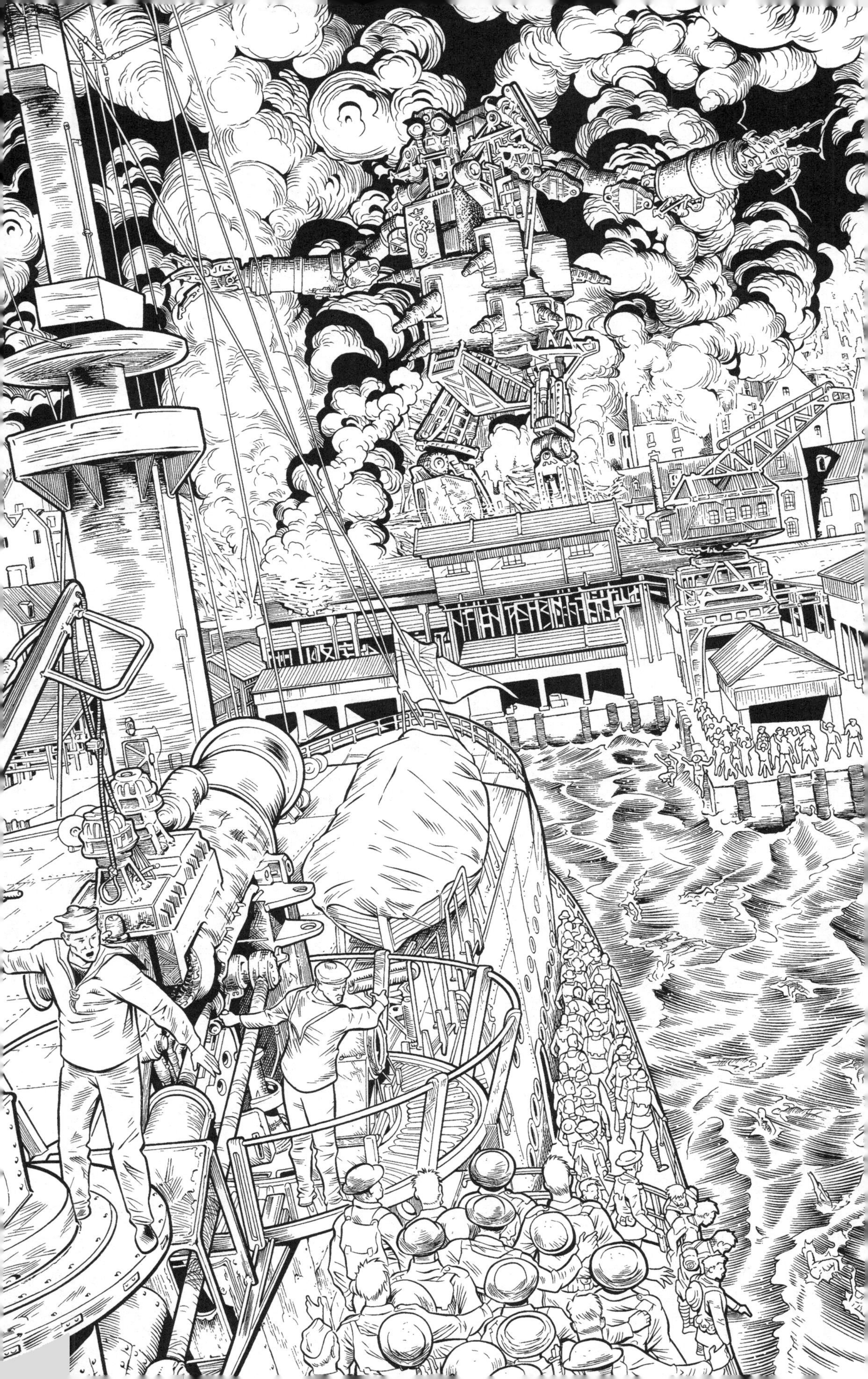

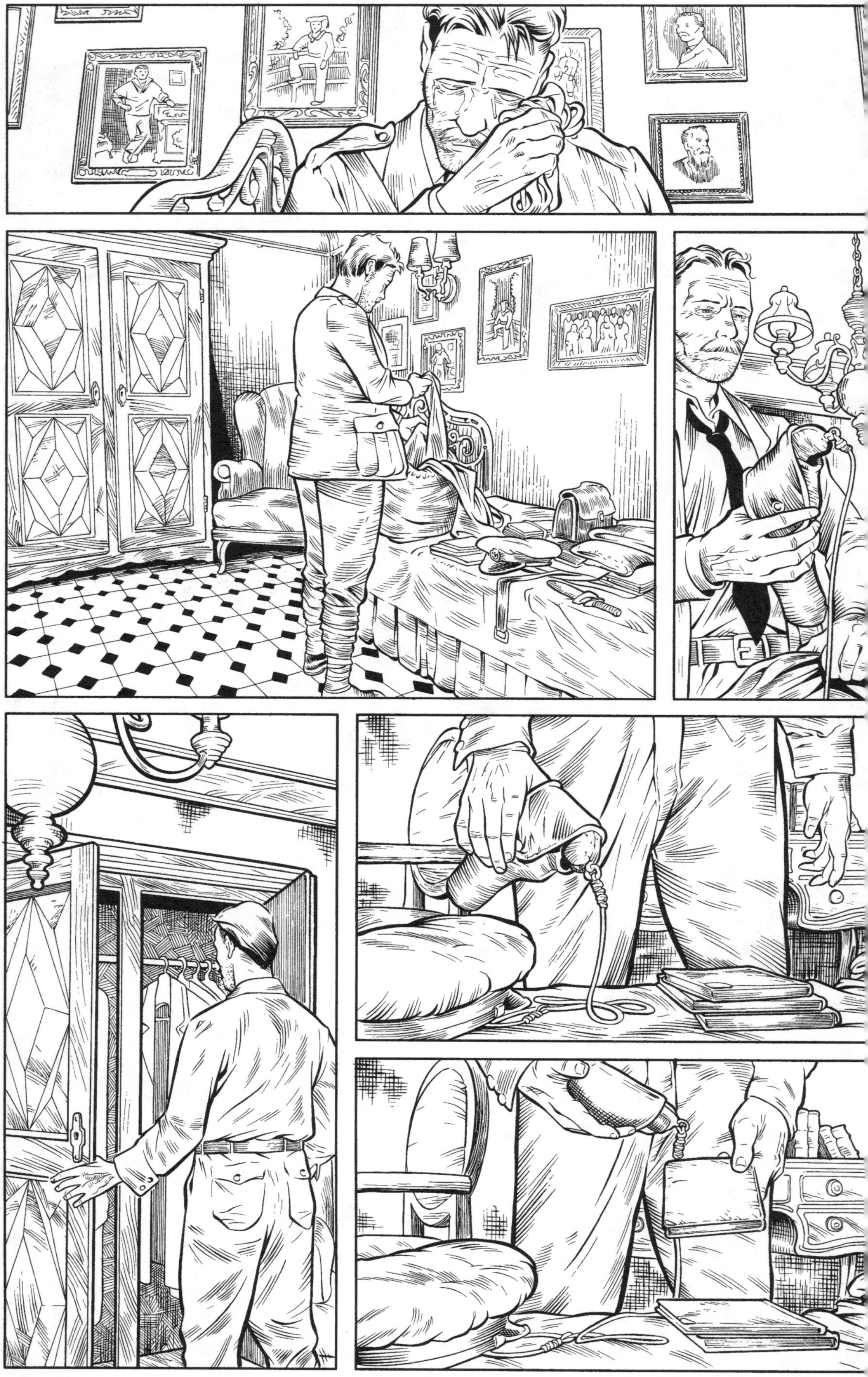

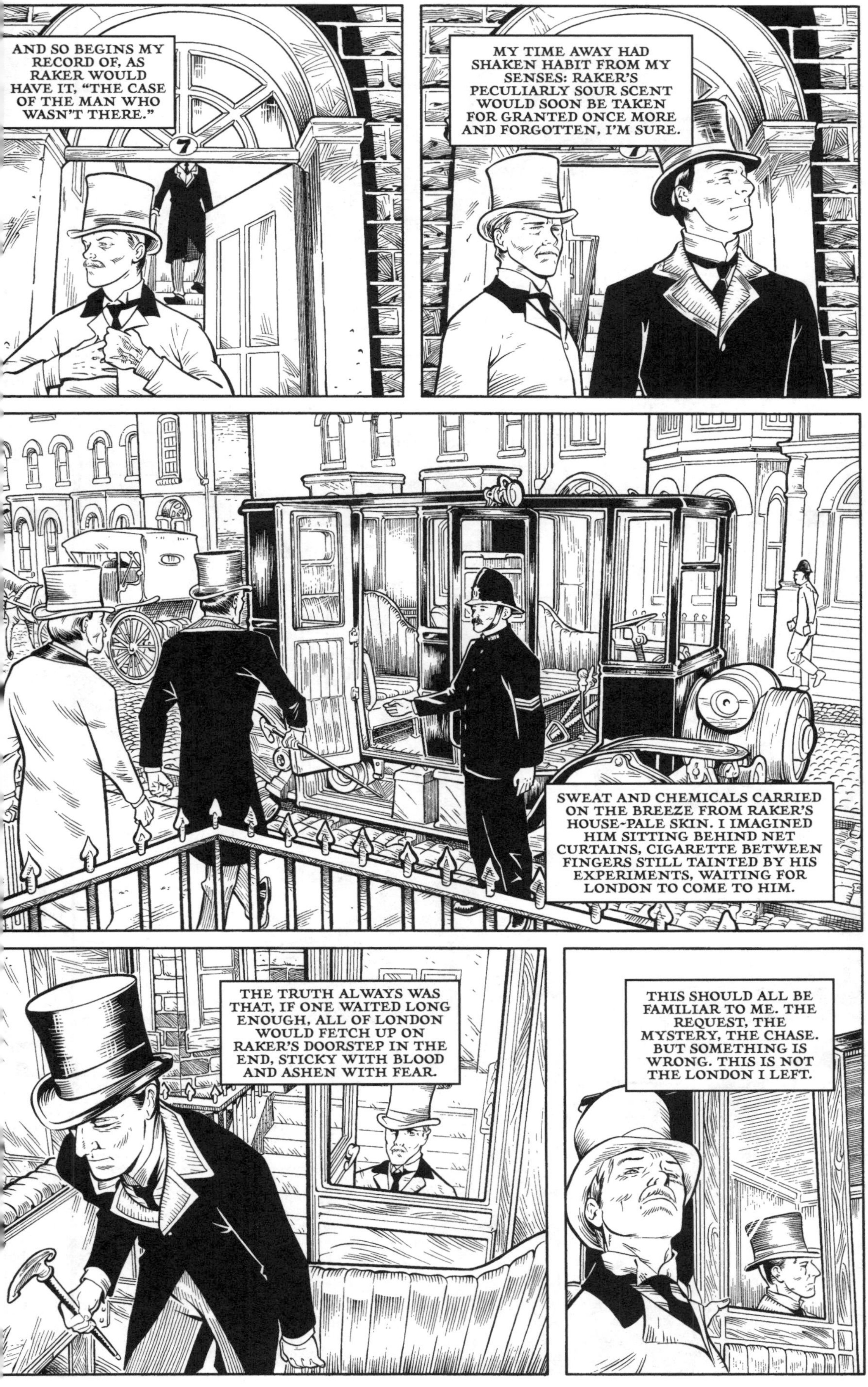
AND SO BEGINS MY RECORD OF, AS RAKER WOULD HAVE IT, "THE CASE OF THE MAN WHO WASN'T THERE."
7
MY TIME AWAY HAD SHAKEN HABIT FROM MY SENSES: RAKER'S PECULIARLY SOUR SCENT WOULD SOON BE TAKEN FOR GRANTED ONCE MORE AND FORGOTTEN, I'M SURE.
SWEAT AND CHEMICALS CARRIED ON THE BREEZE FROM RAKER'S HOUSE-PALE SKIN. I IMAGINED HIM SITTING BEHIND NET CURTAINS, CIGARETTE BETWEEN FINGERS STILL TAINTED BY HIS EXPERIMENTS, WAITING FOR LONDON TO COME TO HIM.
THE TRUTH ALWAYS WAS THAT, IF ONE WAITED LONG ENOUGH, ALL OF LONDON WOULD FETCH UP ON RAKER'S DOORSTEP IN THE END, STICKY WITH BLOOD AND ASHEN WITH FEAR.
THIS SHOULD ALL BE FAMILIAR TO ME. THE REQUEST, THE MYSTERY, THE CHASE. BUT SOMETHING IS WRONG. THIS IS NOT THE LONDON I LEFT.

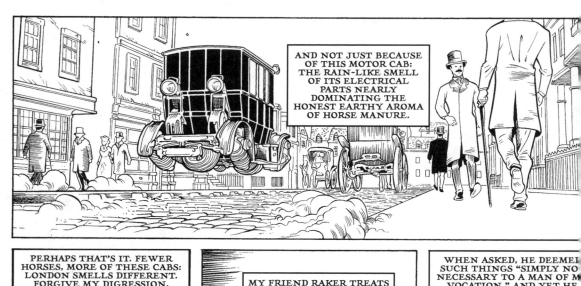

AND NOT JUST BECAUSE OF THIS MOTOR CAB: THE RAIN-LIKE SMELL OF ITS ELECTRICAL PARTS NEARLY DOMINATING THE HONEST EARTHY AROMA OF HORSE MANURE.

PERHAPS THAT'S IT. FEWER HORSES, MORE OF THESE CABS: LONDON SMELLS DIFFERENT. FORGIVE MY DIGRESSION, READER. THESE THINGS WEIGH HEAVY ON AN OLD SOLDIER.

MY FRIEND RAKER TREATS ALMOST EVERY EVENT OF TRANSPORTATION LIKE A SUNDAY OUTING IN JUNE. HE CANNOT RIDE OR DRIVE, AND THE OPERATION OF A BICYCLE COMES MORE NATURALLY TO CRABS THAN TO HE.

WHEN ASKED, HE DEEME[] SUCH THINGS "SIMPLY NO[] NECESSARY TO A MAN OF M[] VOCATION." AND YET HE SMILES, EVERY TIME HE TRAVELS LONDON, AS IF GIFTED A RIDE ON A MAGI[] CARPET.

SO, WATCHAM. WHAT WOULD YOU HAVE ME KNOW OF YOUR WAR?

"MY WAR," HE SAYS, AS IF IT WERE NOT HIS OWN. IN RAKER'S MIND, WAR AND POLITICS ARE CHILDREN'S GAMES, AND THE BALLET OF CRIME THE SOLE INTELLECTUAL PROVINCE OF THE ADULT.

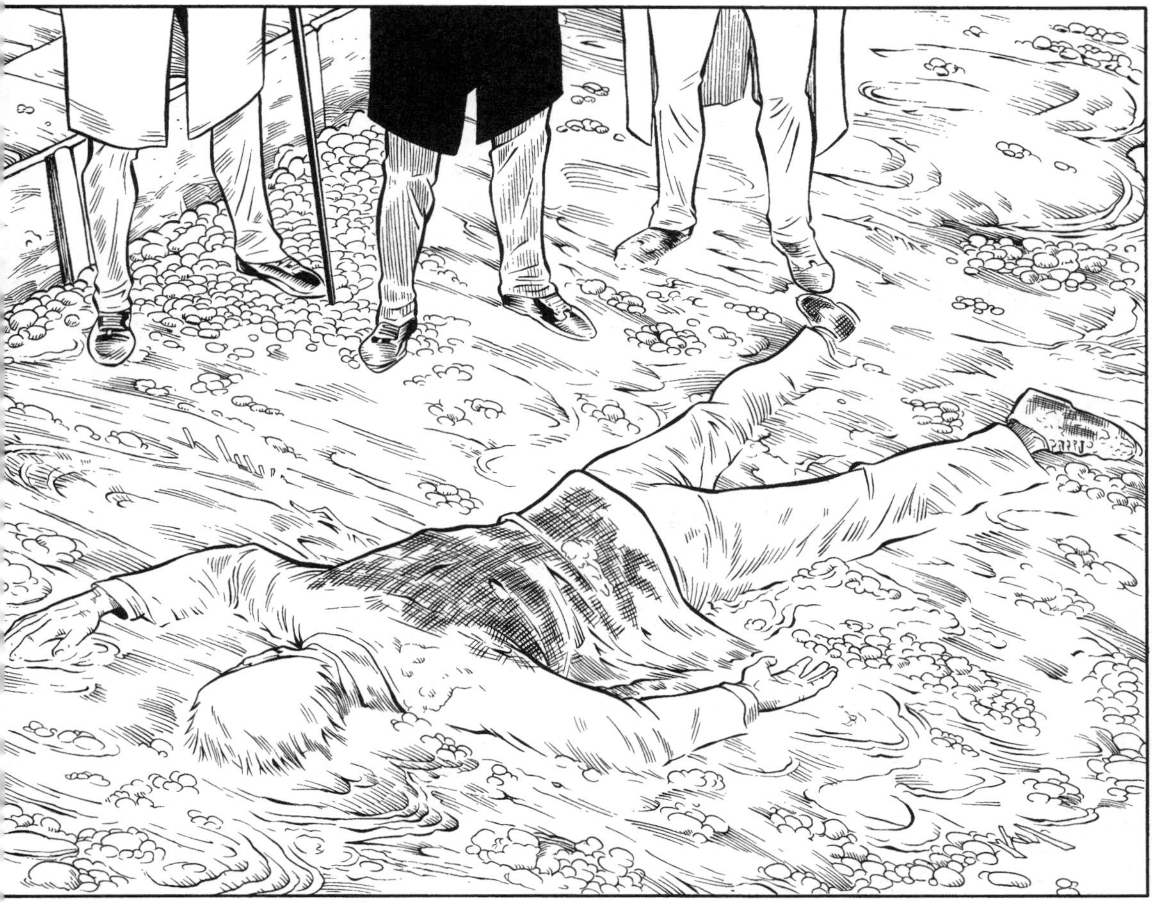

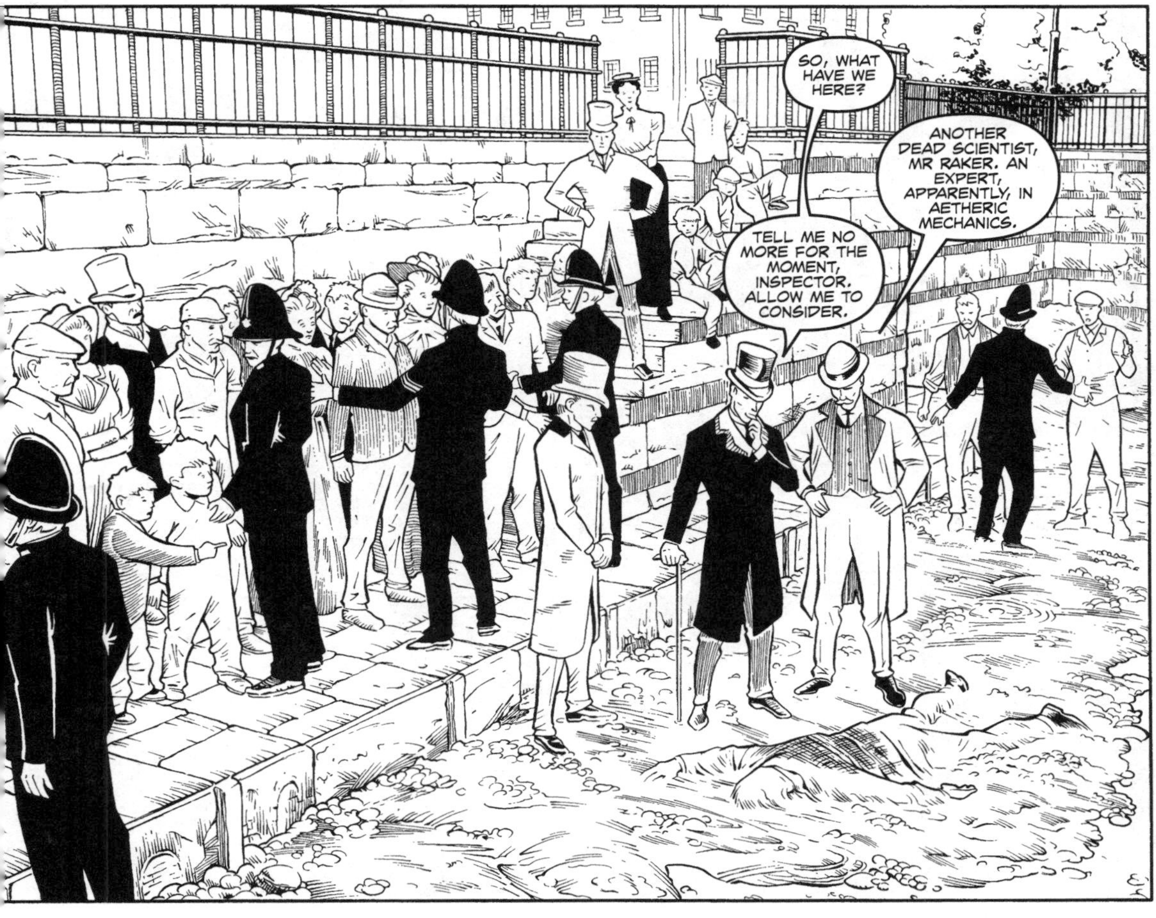
SO, WHAT HAVE WE HERE?
ANOTHER DEAD SCIENTIST, MR RAKER. AN EXPERT, APPARENTLY, IN AETHERIC MECHANICS.
TELL ME NO MORE FOR THE MOMENT, INSPECTOR. ALLOW ME TO CONSIDER.

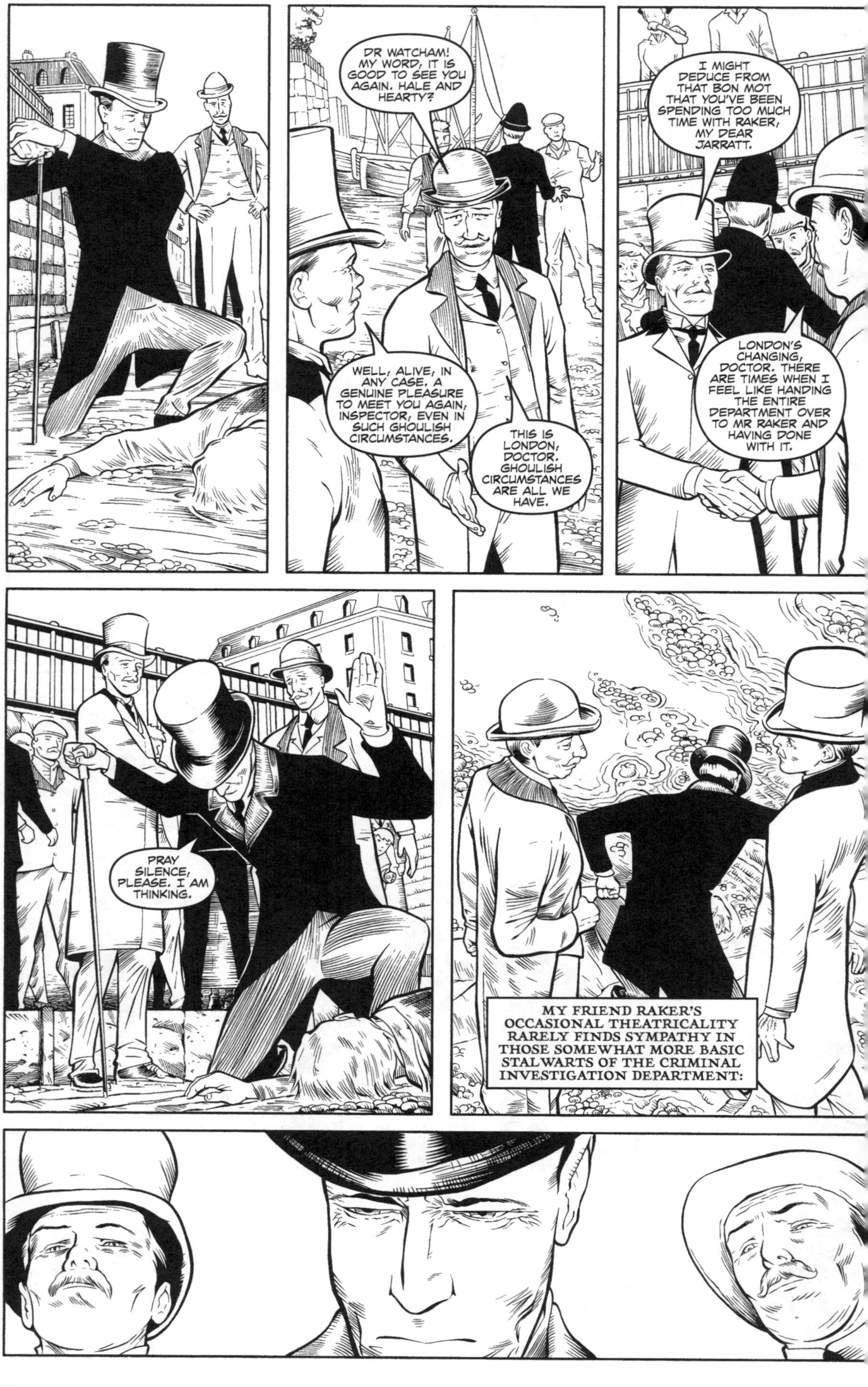
DR WATCHAM! MY WORD, IT IS GOOD TO SEE YOU AGAIN. HALE AND HEARTY?
WELL, ALIVE, IN ANY CASE. A GENUINE PLEASURE TO MEET YOU AGAIN, INSPECTOR, EVEN IN SUCH GHOULISH CIRCUMSTANCES.
THIS IS LONDON, DOCTOR. GHOULISH CIRCUMSTANCES ARE ALL WE HAVE.
I MIGHT DEDUCE FROM THAT BON MOT THAT YOU'VE BEEN SPENDING TOO MUCH TIME WITH RAKER, MY DEAR JARRATT.
LONDON'S CHANGING, DOCTOR. THERE ARE TIMES WHEN I FEEL LIKE HANDING THE ENTIRE DEPARTMENT OVER TO MR RAKER AND HAVING DONE WITH IT.
PRAY SILENCE, PLEASE. I AM THINKING.
MY FRIEND RAKER'S OCCASIONAL THEATRICALITY RARELY FINDS SYMPATHY IN THOSE SOMEWHAT MORE BASIC STALWARTS OF THE CRIMINAL INVESTIGATION DEPARTMENT:

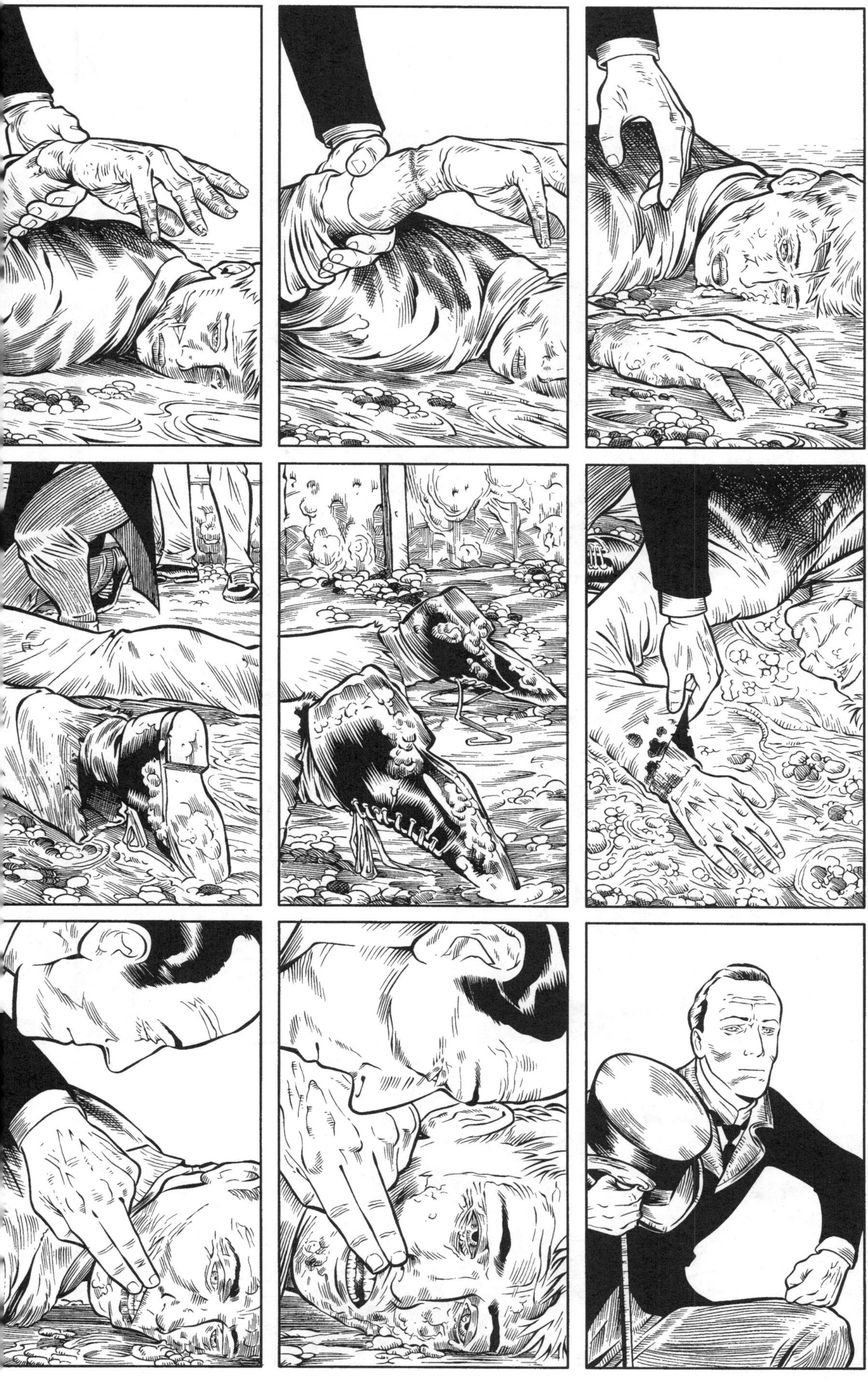

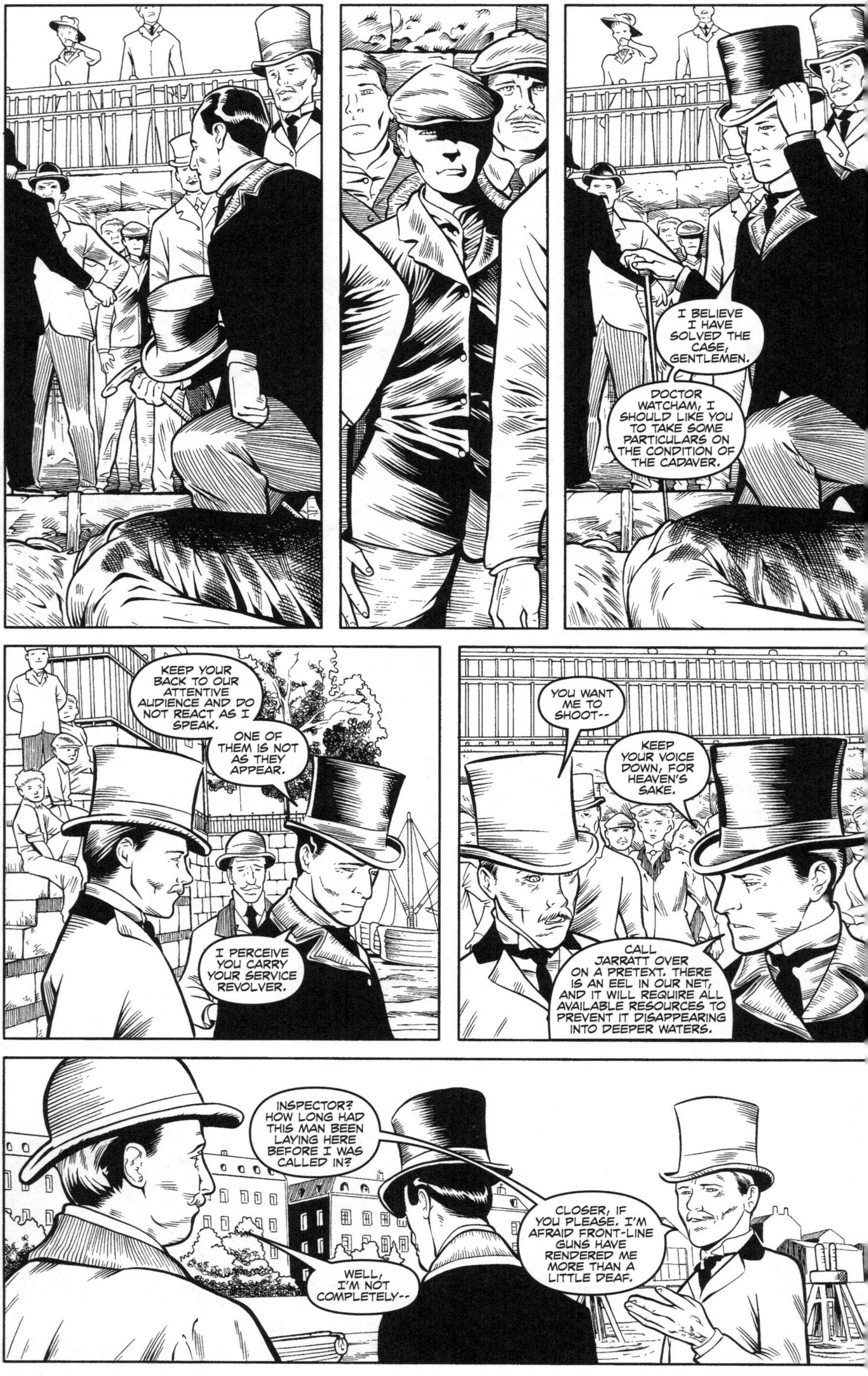
I BELIEVE I HAVE SOLVED THE CASE, GENTLEMEN.
DOCTOR WATCHAM, I SHOULD LIKE YOU TO TAKE SOME PARTICULARS ON THE CONDITION OF THE CADAVER.
KEEP YOUR BACK TO OUR ATTENTIVE AUDIENCE AND DO NOT REACT AS I SPEAK.
ONE OF THEM IS NOT AS THEY APPEAR.
I PERCEIVE YOU CARRY YOUR SERVICE REVOLVER.
YOU WANT ME TO SHOOT--
KEEP YOUR VOICE DOWN, FOR HEAVEN'S SAKE.
CALL JARRATT OVER ON A PRETEXT. THERE IS AN EEL IN OUR NET, AND IT WILL REQUIRE ALL AVAILABLE RESOURCES TO PREVENT IT DISAPPEARING INTO DEEPER WATERS.
INSPECTOR? HOW LONG HAD THIS MAN BEEN LAYING HERE BEFORE I WAS CALLED IN?
WELL, I'M NOT COMPLETELY--
CLOSER, IF YOU PLEASE. I'M AFRAID FRONT-LINE GUNS HAVE RENDERED ME MORE THAN A LITTLE DEAF.

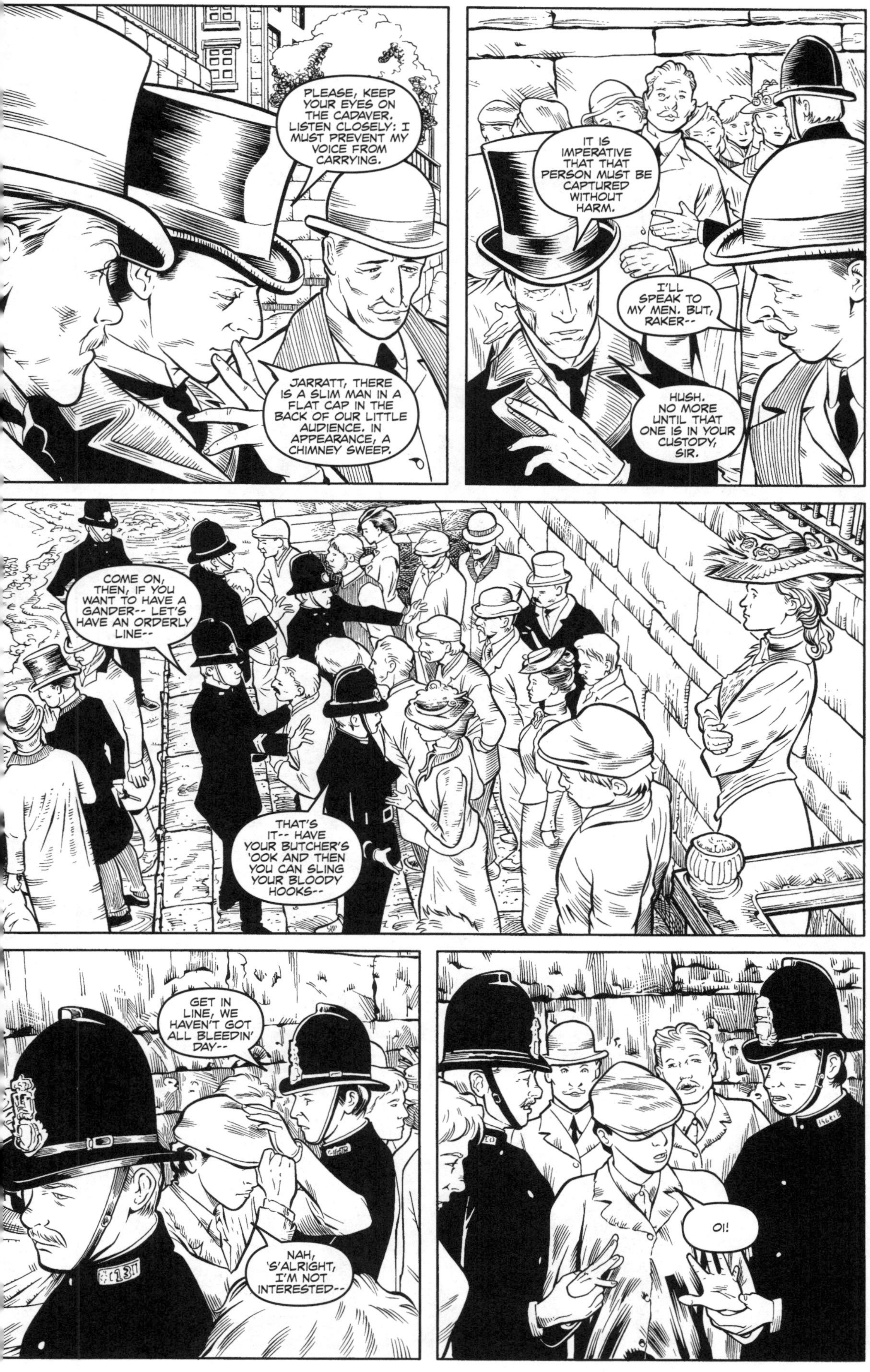
PLEASE, KEEP YOUR EYES ON THE CADAVER. LISTEN CLOSELY: I MUST PREVENT MY VOICE FROM CARRYING.
JARRATT, THERE IS A SLIM MAN IN A FLAT CAP IN THE BACK OF OUR LITTLE AUDIENCE. IN APPEARANCE, A CHIMNEY SWEEP.
IT IS IMPERATIVE THAT THAT PERSON MUST BE CAPTURED WITHOUT HARM.
I'LL SPEAK TO MY MEN. BUT, RAKER--
HUSH. NO MORE UNTIL THAT ONE IS IN YOUR CUSTODY, SIR.
COME ON, THEN, IF YOU WANT TO HAVE A GANDER-- LET'S HAVE AN ORDERLY LINE--
THAT'S IT-- HAVE YOUR BUTCHER'S 'OOK AND THEN YOU CAN SLING YOUR BLOODY HOOKS--
GET IN LINE, WE HAVEN'T GOT ALL BLEEDIN' DAY--
NAH, 'S'ALRIGHT, I'M NOT INTERESTED--
OI!

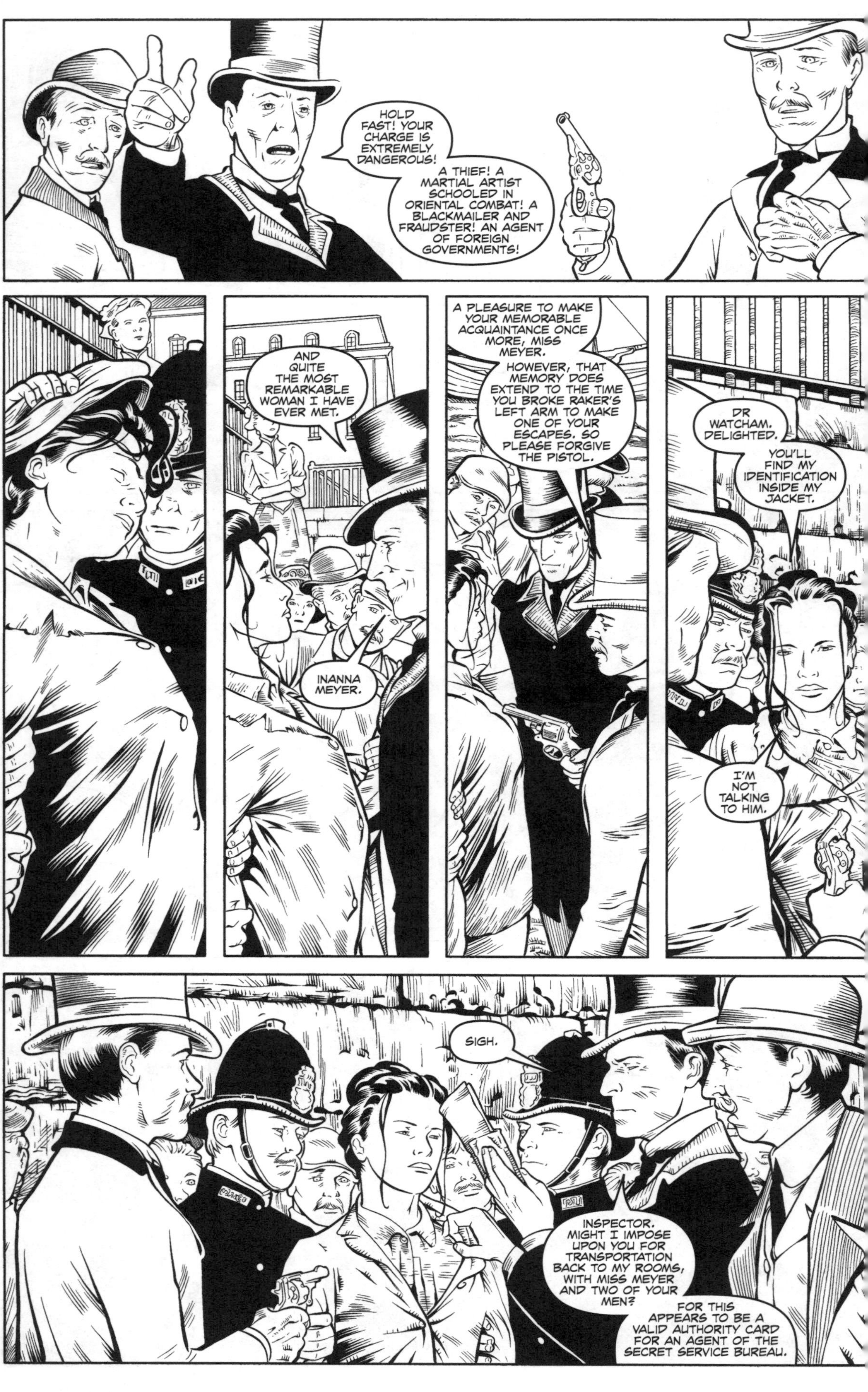
HOLD FAST! YOUR CHARGE IS EXTREMELY DANGEROUS!
A THIEF! A MARTIAL ARTIST SCHOOLED IN ORIENTAL COMBAT! A BLACKMAILER AND FRAUDSTER! AN AGENT OF FOREIGN GOVERNMENTS!
AND QUITE THE MOST REMARKABLE WOMAN I HAVE EVER MET.
INANNA MEYER.
A PLEASURE TO MAKE YOUR MEMORABLE ACQUAINTANCE ONCE MORE, MISS MEYER.
HOWEVER, THAT MEMORY DOES EXTEND TO THE TIME YOU BROKE RAKER'S LEFT ARM TO MAKE ONE OF YOUR ESCAPES. SO PLEASE FORGIVE THE PISTOL.
DR WATCHAM. DELIGHTED.
YOU'LL FIND MY IDENTIFICATION INSIDE MY JACKET.
I'M NOT TALKING TO HIM.
SIGH.
INSPECTOR. MIGHT I IMPOSE UPON YOU FOR TRANSPORTATION BACK TO MY ROOMS, WITH MISS MEYER AND TWO OF YOUR MEN?
FOR THIS APPEARS TO BE A VALID AUTHORITY CARD FOR AN AGENT OF THE SECRET SERVICE BUREAU.

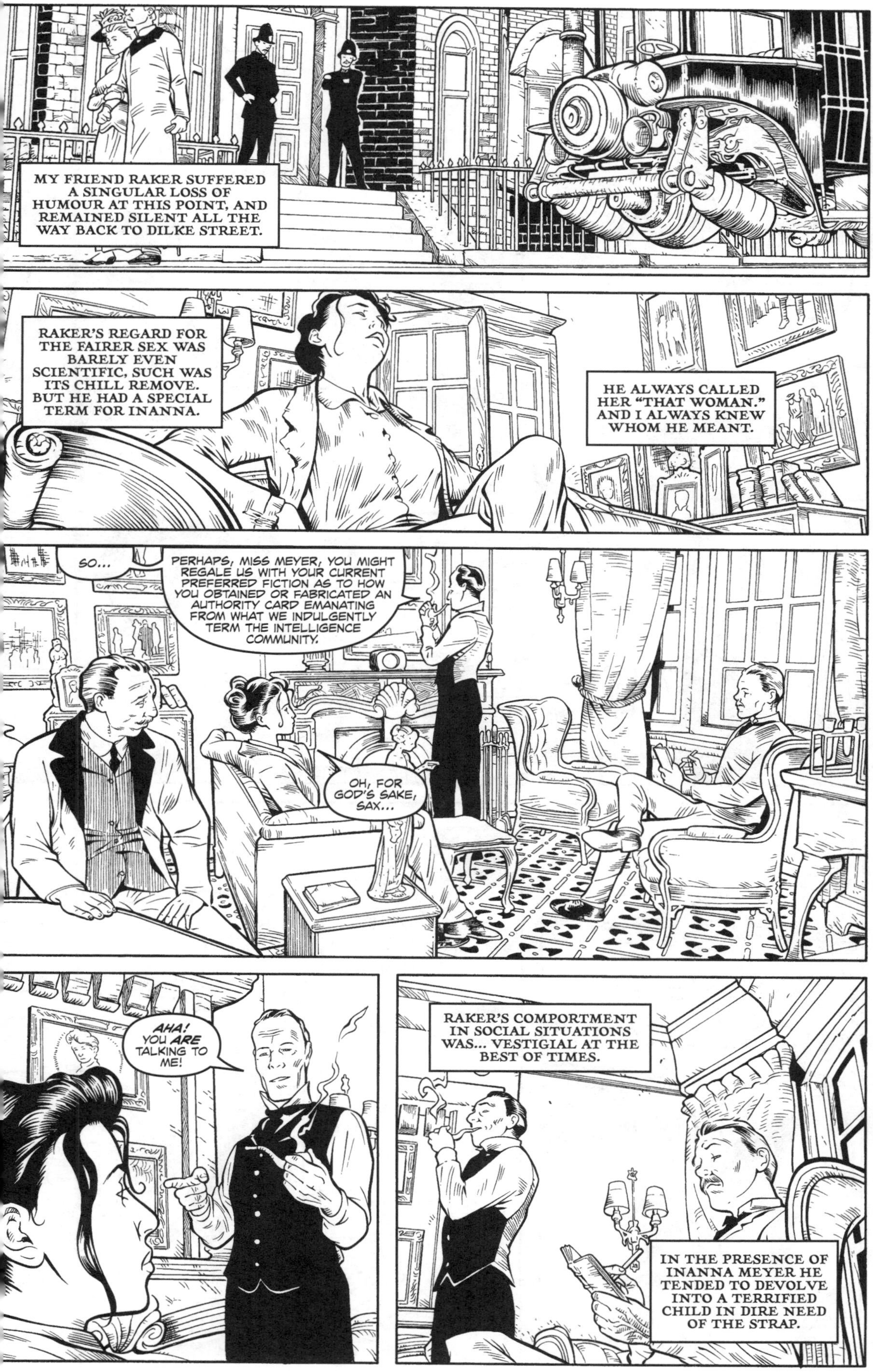
MY FRIEND RAKER SUFFERED A SINGULAR LOSS OF HUMOUR AT THIS POINT, AND REMAINED SILENT ALL THE WAY BACK TO DILKE STREET.
RAKER'S REGARD FOR THE FAIRER SEX WAS BARELY EVEN SCIENTIFIC, SUCH WAS ITS CHILL REMOVE. BUT HE HAD A SPECIAL TERM FOR INANNA.
HE ALWAYS CALLED HER "THAT WOMAN." AND I ALWAYS KNEW WHOM HE MEANT.
SO...
PERHAPS, MISS MEYER, YOU MIGHT REGALE US WITH YOUR CURRENT PREFERRED FICTION AS TO HOW YOU OBTAINED OR FABRICATED AN AUTHORITY CARD EMANATING FROM WHAT WE INDULGENTLY TERM THE INTELLIGENCE COMMUNITY.
OH, FOR GOD'S SAKE, SAX...
AHA! YOU ARE TALKING TO ME!
RAKER'S COMPORTMENT IN SOCIAL SITUATIONS WAS... VESTIGIAL AT THE BEST OF TIMES.
IN THE PRESENCE OF INANNA MEYER HE TENDED TO DEVOLVE INTO A TERRIFIED CHILD IN DIRE NEED OF THE STRAP.

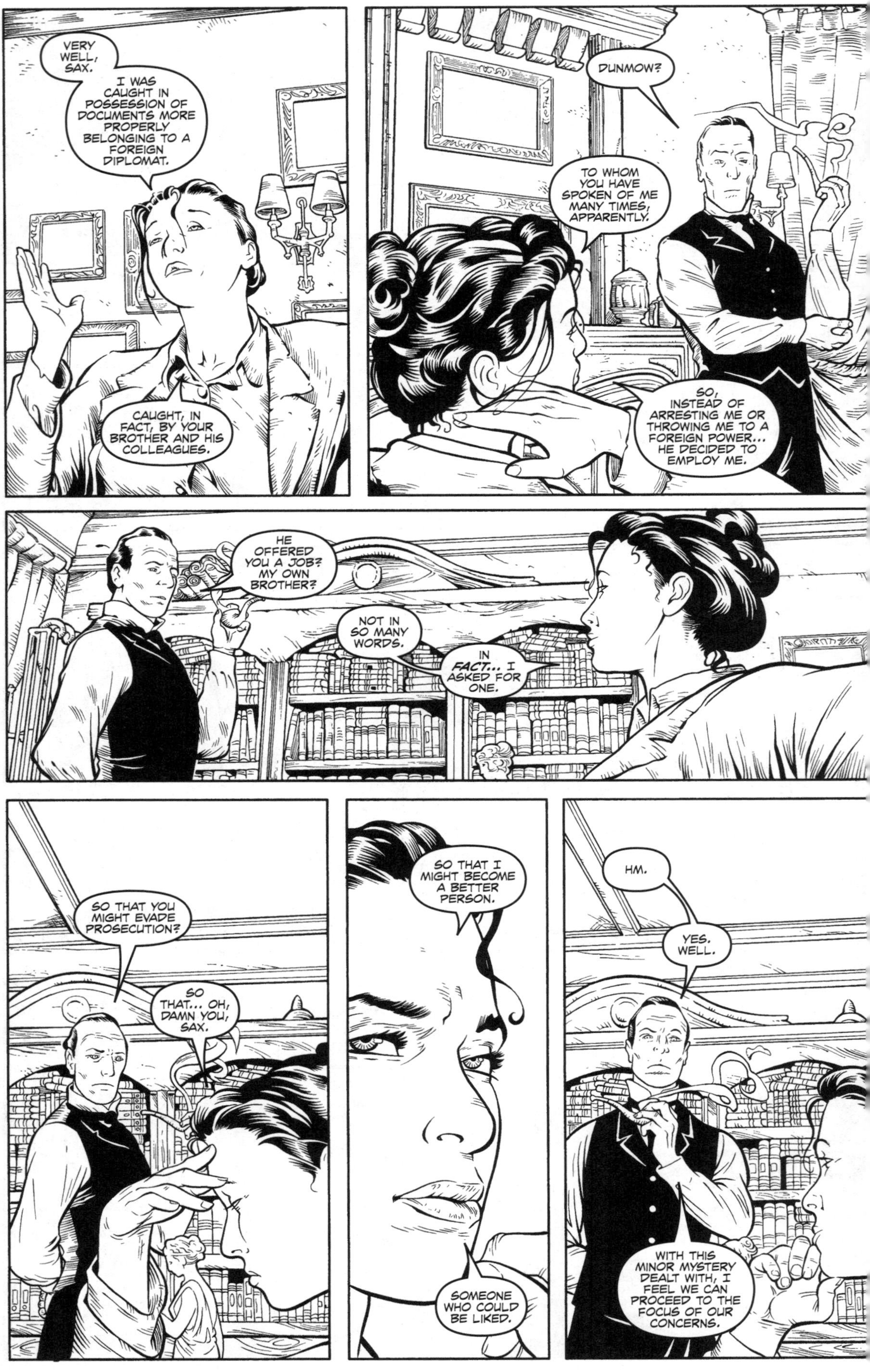
VERY WELL, SAX.
I WAS CAUGHT IN POSSESSION OF DOCUMENTS MORE PROPERLY BELONGING TO A FOREIGN DIPLOMAT.
CAUGHT, IN FACT, BY YOUR BROTHER AND HIS COLLEAGUES.
DUNMOW?
TO WHOM YOU HAVE SPOKEN OF ME MANY TIMES, APPARENTLY.
SO, INSTEAD OF ARRESTING ME OR THROWING ME TO A FOREIGN POWER... HE DECIDED TO EMPLOY ME.
HE OFFERED YOU A JOB? MY OWN BROTHER?
NOT IN SO MANY WORDS.
IN *FACT*... I ASKED FOR ONE.
SO THAT YOU MIGHT EVADE PROSECUTION?
SO THAT... OH, DAMN YOU, SAX.
SO THAT I MIGHT BECOME A BETTER PERSON.
SOMEONE WHO COULD BE LIKED.
HM.
YES. WELL.
WITH THIS MINOR MYSTERY DEALT WITH, I FEEL WE CAN PROCEED TO THE FOCUS OF OUR CONCERNS.

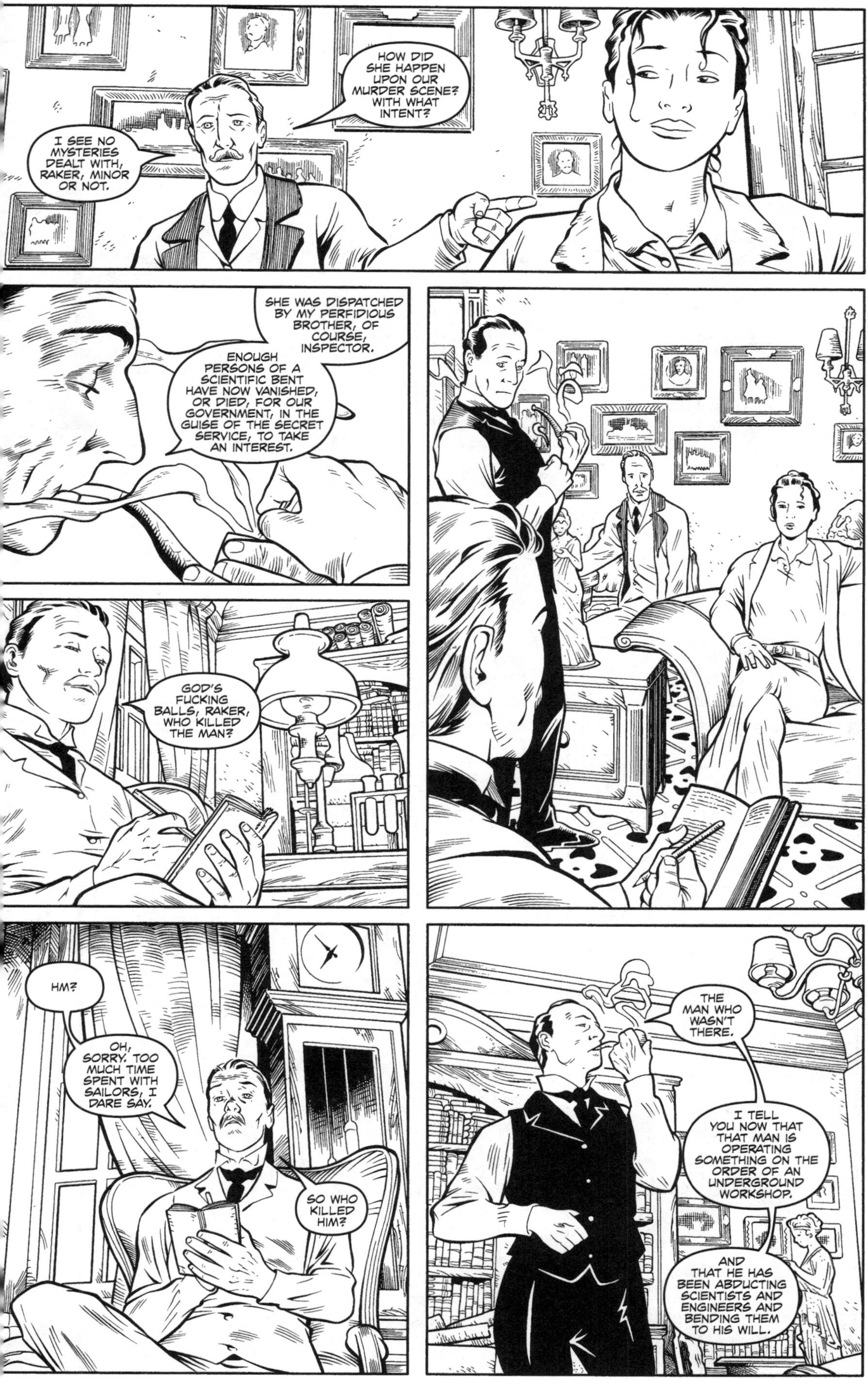

I SEE NO MYSTERIES DEALT WITH, RAKER, MINOR OR NOT.
HOW DID SHE HAPPEN UPON OUR MURDER SCENE? WITH WHAT INTENT?
SHE WAS DISPATCHED BY MY PERFIDIOUS BROTHER, OF COURSE, INSPECTOR.
ENOUGH PERSONS OF A SCIENTIFIC BENT HAVE NOW VANISHED, OR DIED, FOR OUR GOVERNMENT, IN THE GUISE OF THE SECRET SERVICE, TO TAKE AN INTEREST.
GOD'S FUCKING BALLS, RAKER, WHO KILLED THE MAN?
HM?
OH, SORRY. TOO MUCH TIME SPENT WITH SAILORS, I DARE SAY.
SO WHO KILLED HIM?
THE MAN WHO WASN'T THERE.
I TELL YOU NOW THAT THAT MAN IS OPERATING SOMETHING ON THE ORDER OF AN UNDERGROUND WORKSHOP.
AND THAT HE HAS BEEN ABDUCTING SCIENTISTS AND ENGINEERS AND BENDING THEM TO HIS WILL.

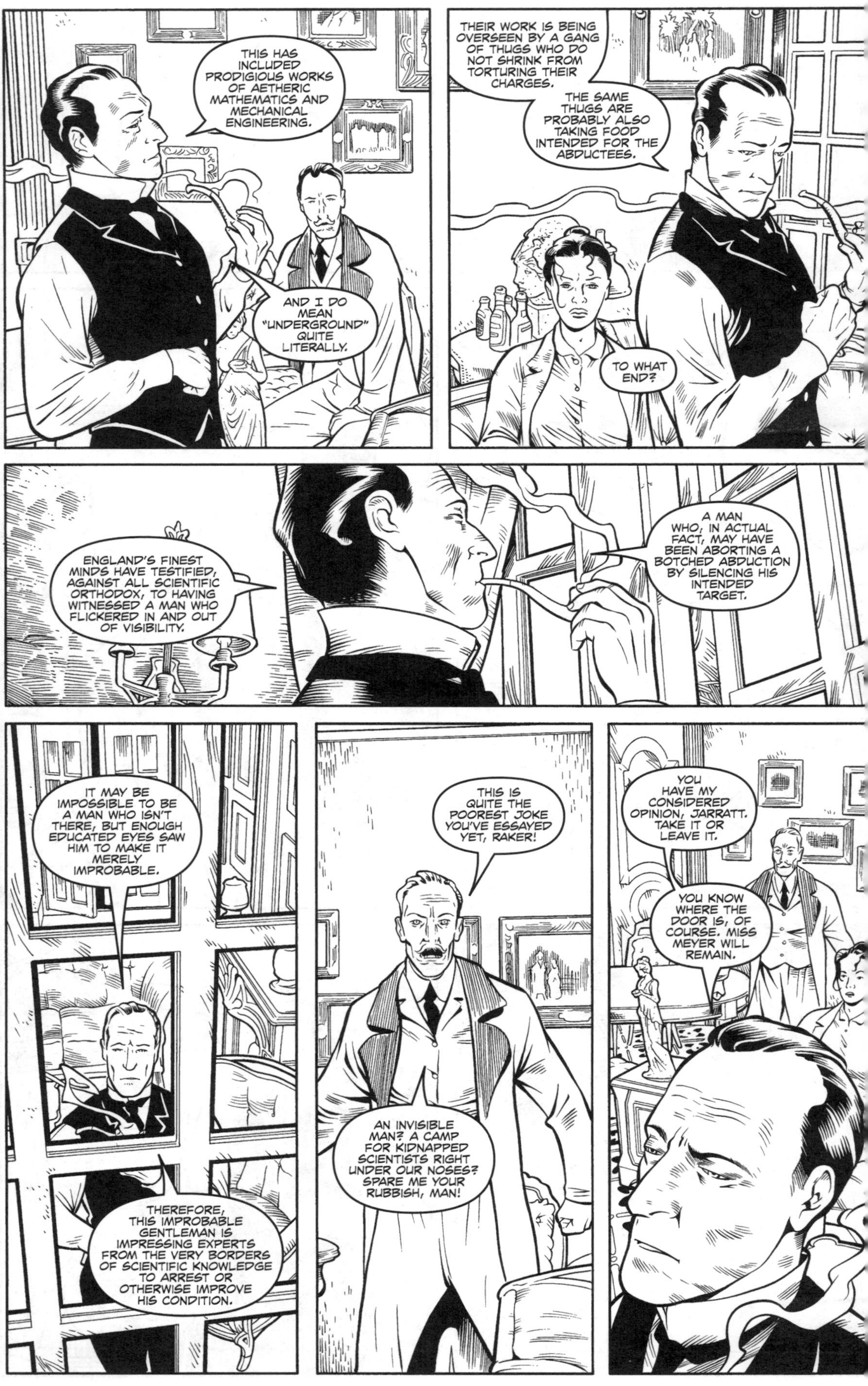
THIS HAS INCLUDED PRODIGIOUS WORKS OF AETHERIC MATHEMATICS AND MECHANICAL ENGINEERING.
AND I DO MEAN "UNDERGROUND" QUITE LITERALLY.
THEIR WORK IS BEING OVERSEEN BY A GANG OF THUGS WHO DO NOT SHRINK FROM TORTURING THEIR CHARGES.
THE SAME THUGS ARE PROBABLY ALSO TAKING FOOD INTENDED FOR THE ABDUCTEES.
TO WHAT END?
ENGLAND'S FINEST MINDS HAVE TESTIFIED, AGAINST ALL SCIENTIFIC ORTHODOX, TO HAVING WITNESSED A MAN WHO FLICKERED IN AND OUT OF VISIBILITY.
A MAN WHO, IN ACTUAL FACT, MAY HAVE BEEN ABORTING A BOTCHED ABDUCTION BY SILENCING HIS INTENDED TARGET.
IT MAY BE IMPOSSIBLE TO BE A MAN WHO ISN'T THERE, BUT ENOUGH EDUCATED EYES SAW HIM TO MAKE IT MERELY IMPROBABLE.
THEREFORE, THIS IMPROBABLE GENTLEMAN IS IMPRESSING EXPERTS FROM THE VERY BORDERS OF SCIENTIFIC KNOWLEDGE TO ARREST OR OTHERWISE IMPROVE HIS CONDITION.
THIS IS QUITE THE POOREST JOKE YOU'VE ESSAYED YET, RAKER!
AN INVISIBLE MAN? A CAMP FOR KIDNAPPED SCIENTISTS RIGHT UNDER OUR NOSES? SPARE ME YOUR RUBBISH, MAN!
YOU HAVE MY CONSIDERED OPINION, JARRATT. TAKE IT OR LEAVE IT.
YOU KNOW WHERE THE DOOR IS, OF COURSE. MISS MEYER WILL REMAIN.

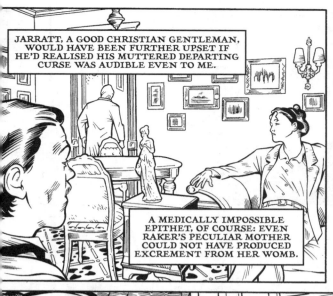

JARRATT, A GOOD CHRISTIAN GENTLEMAN, WOULD HAVE BEEN FURTHER UPSET IF HE'D REALISED HIS MUTTERED DEPARTING CURSE WAS AUDIBLE EVEN TO ME.

A MEDICALLY IMPOSSIBLE EPITHET, OF COURSE: EVEN RAKER'S PECULIAR MOTHER COULD NOT HAVE PRODUCED EXCREMENT FROM HER WOMB.

YOU SHOULD NOT TASK THE POOR MAN LIKE THAT, SAX.

HE'S ONLY TRYING TO DO HIS JOB. AND IT'S HARD ENOUGH TO BE A LONDON COPPER IN THE BEST OF DAYS.

AND ARE THESE NOT THE BEST OF DAYS?

A MASTER CRIMINAL AFFLICTED BY SOME DISEASE THAT NEAR BEGGARS COMPREHENSION, OPERATING A SLAVE CAMP FOR THE BRILLIANT UNDER LONDON'S VERY STREETS?

TO TEST OUR METTLE AGAINST A MIND LIKE THAT? THESE ARE SURELY THE GREAT DAYS OF OUR LIVES!

EH? EH?

COUGH

AH, SAX. EVEN WHEN IT WAS I YOU WERE PURSUING, I LOVED TO SEE THESE MOMENTS.

WHY DID YOU ASK ME TO STAY?

BECAUSE, IN THE ABSENCE OF JARRATT, I WILL REQUIRE AN ACCREDITED OFFICER OF THE CROWN TO EFFECT THE ARREST, TONIGHT, OF THE MAN WHO WASN'T THERE.

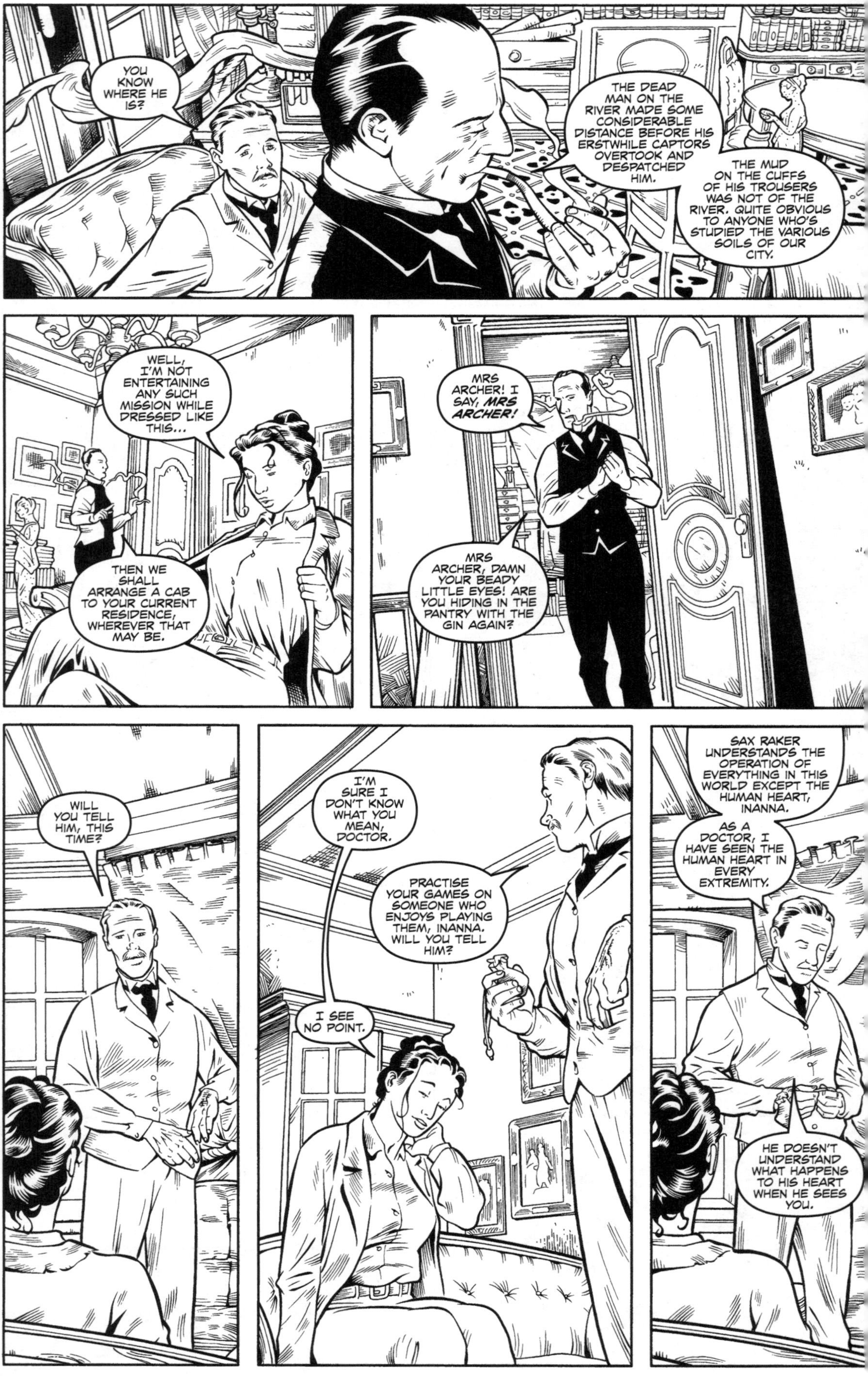
YOU KNOW WHERE HE IS?
THE DEAD MAN ON THE RIVER MADE SOME CONSIDERABLE DISTANCE BEFORE HIS ERSTWHILE CAPTORS OVERTOOK AND DESPATCHED HIM.
THE MUD ON THE CUFFS OF HIS TROUSERS WAS NOT OF THE RIVER. QUITE OBVIOUS TO ANYONE WHO'S STUDIED THE VARIOUS SOILS OF OUR CITY.
WELL, I'M NOT ENTERTAINING ANY SUCH MISSION WHILE DRESSED LIKE THIS...
THEN WE SHALL ARRANGE A CAB TO YOUR CURRENT RESIDENCE, WHEREVER THAT MAY BE.
MRS ARCHER! I SAY, MRS ARCHER!
MRS ARCHER, DAMN YOUR BEADY LITTLE EYES! ARE YOU HIDING IN THE PANTRY WITH THE GIN AGAIN?
WILL YOU TELL HIM, THIS TIME?
I'M SURE I DON'T KNOW WHAT YOU MEAN, DOCTOR.
PRACTISE YOUR GAMES ON SOMEONE WHO ENJOYS PLAYING THEM, INANNA. WILL YOU TELL HIM?
I SEE NO POINT.
SAX RAKER UNDERSTANDS THE OPERATION OF EVERYTHING IN THIS WORLD EXCEPT THE HUMAN HEART, INANNA.
AS A DOCTOR, I HAVE SEEN THE HUMAN HEART IN EVERY EXTREMITY.
HE DOESN'T UNDERSTAND WHAT HAPPENS TO HIS HEART WHEN HE SEES YOU.

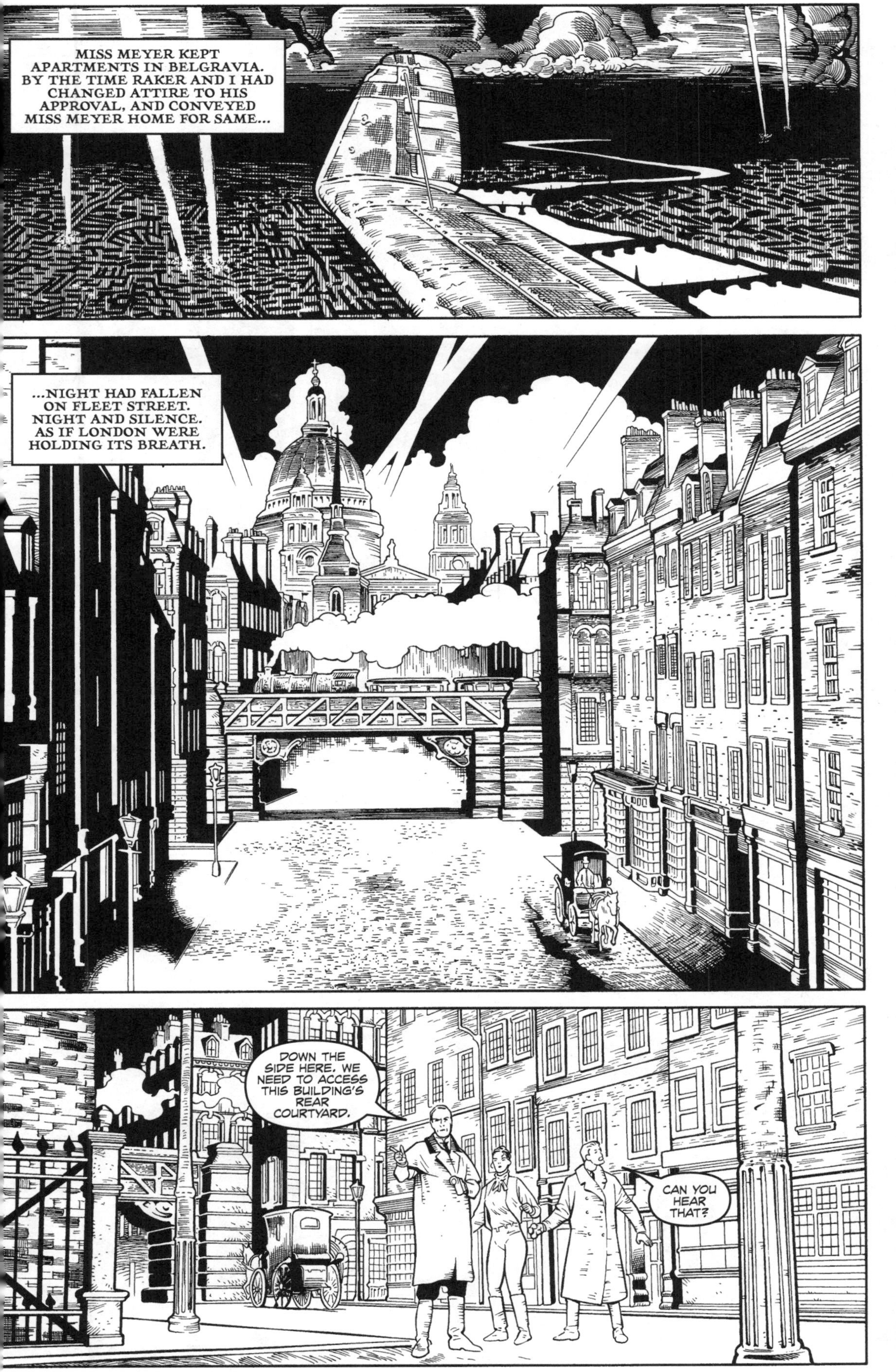
MISS MEYER KEPT APARTMENTS IN BELGRAVIA. BY THE TIME RAKER AND I HAD CHANGED ATTIRE TO HIS APPROVAL, AND CONVEYED MISS MEYER HOME FOR SAME...
...NIGHT HAD FALLEN ON FLEET STREET. NIGHT AND SILENCE. AS IF LONDON WERE HOLDING ITS BREATH.
DOWN THE SIDE HERE. WE NEED TO ACCESS THIS BUILDING'S REAR COURTYARD.
CAN YOU HEAR THAT?

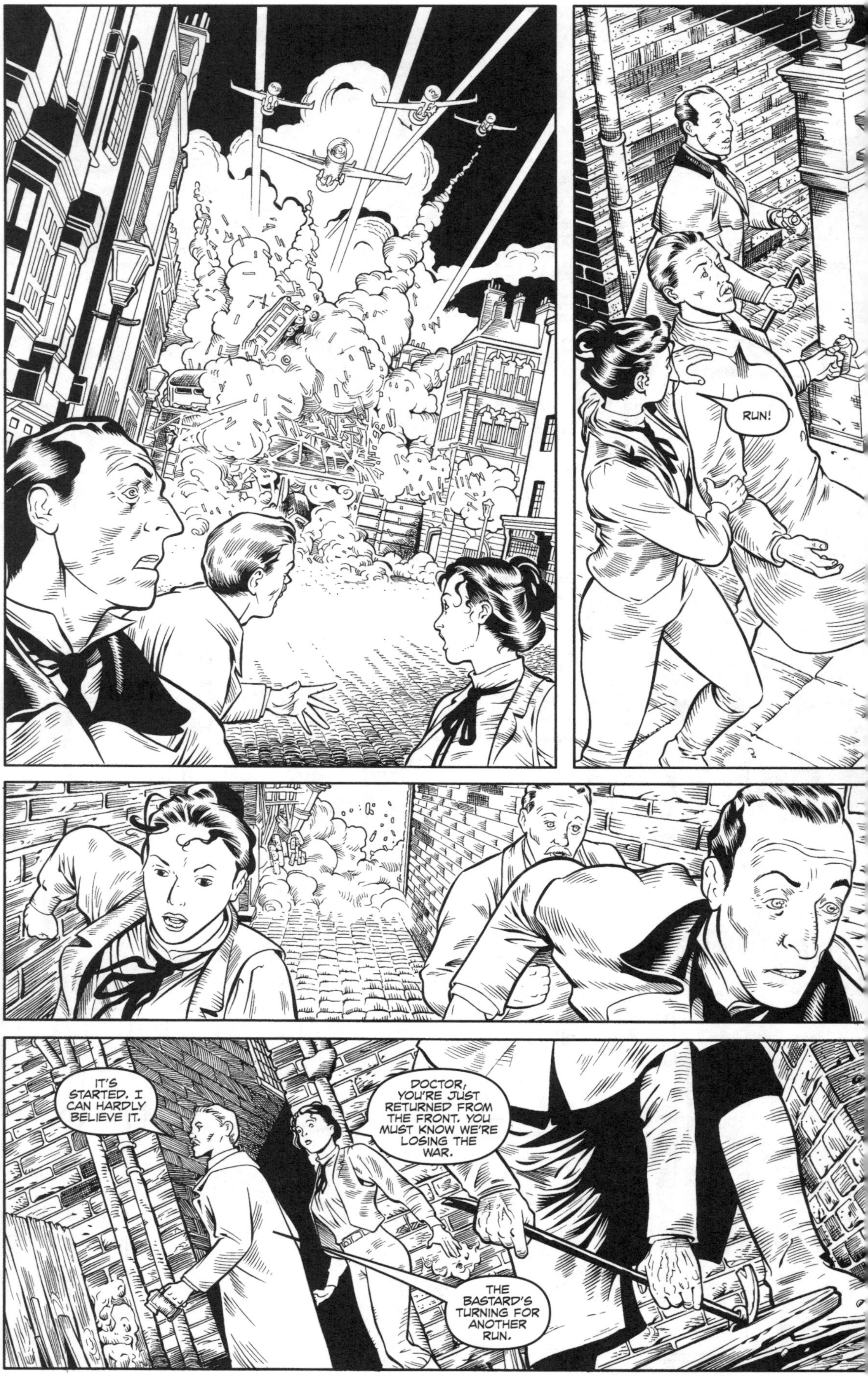
RUN!
IT'S STARTED. I CAN HARDLY BELIEVE IT.
DOCTOR, YOU'RE JUST RETURNED FROM THE FRONT. YOU MUST KNOW WE'RE LOSING THE WAR.
THE BASTARD'S TURNING FOR ANOTHER RUN.

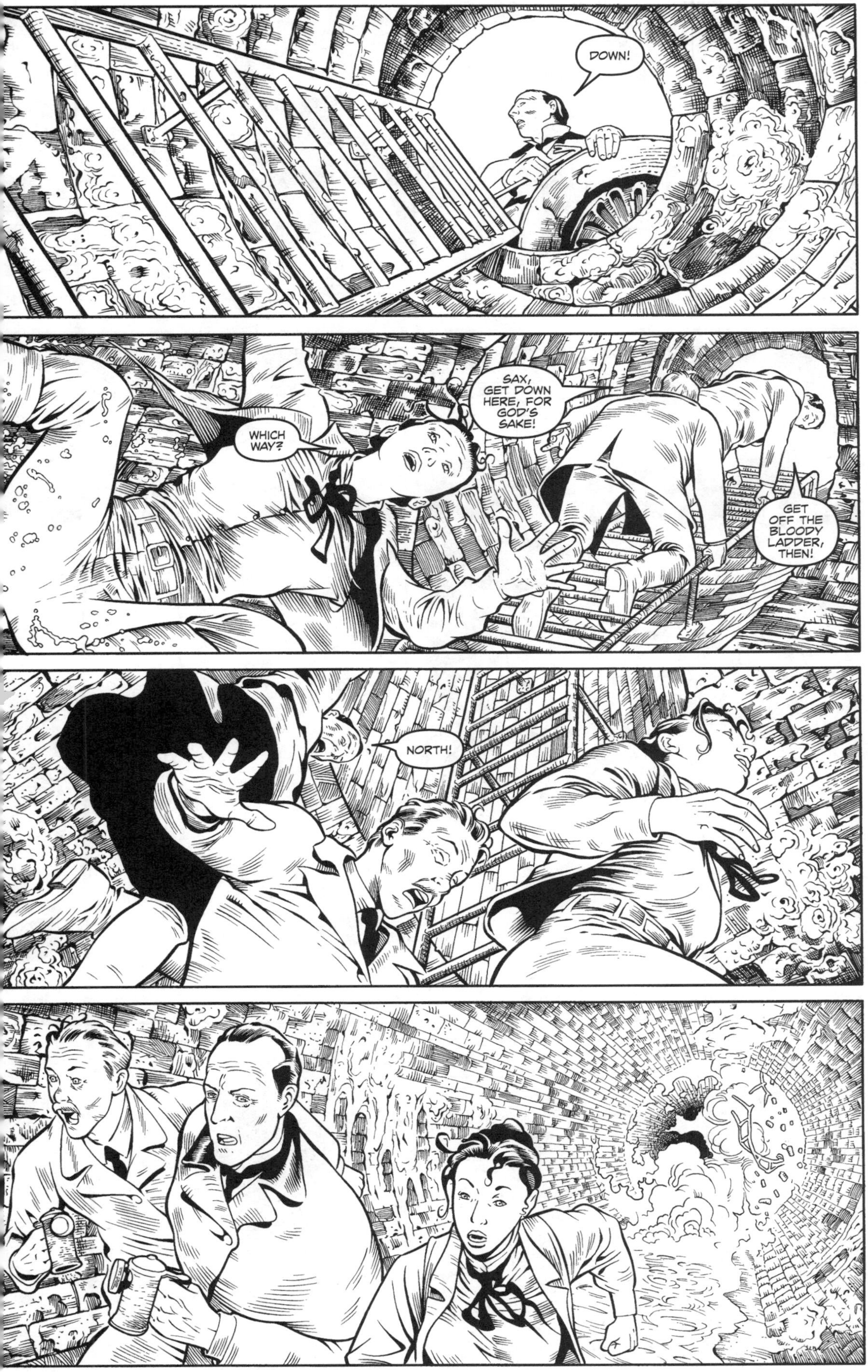
DOWN!
WHICH WAY?
SAX, GET DOWN HERE, FOR GOD'S SAKE!
GET OFF THE BLOODY LADDER, THEN!
NORTH!

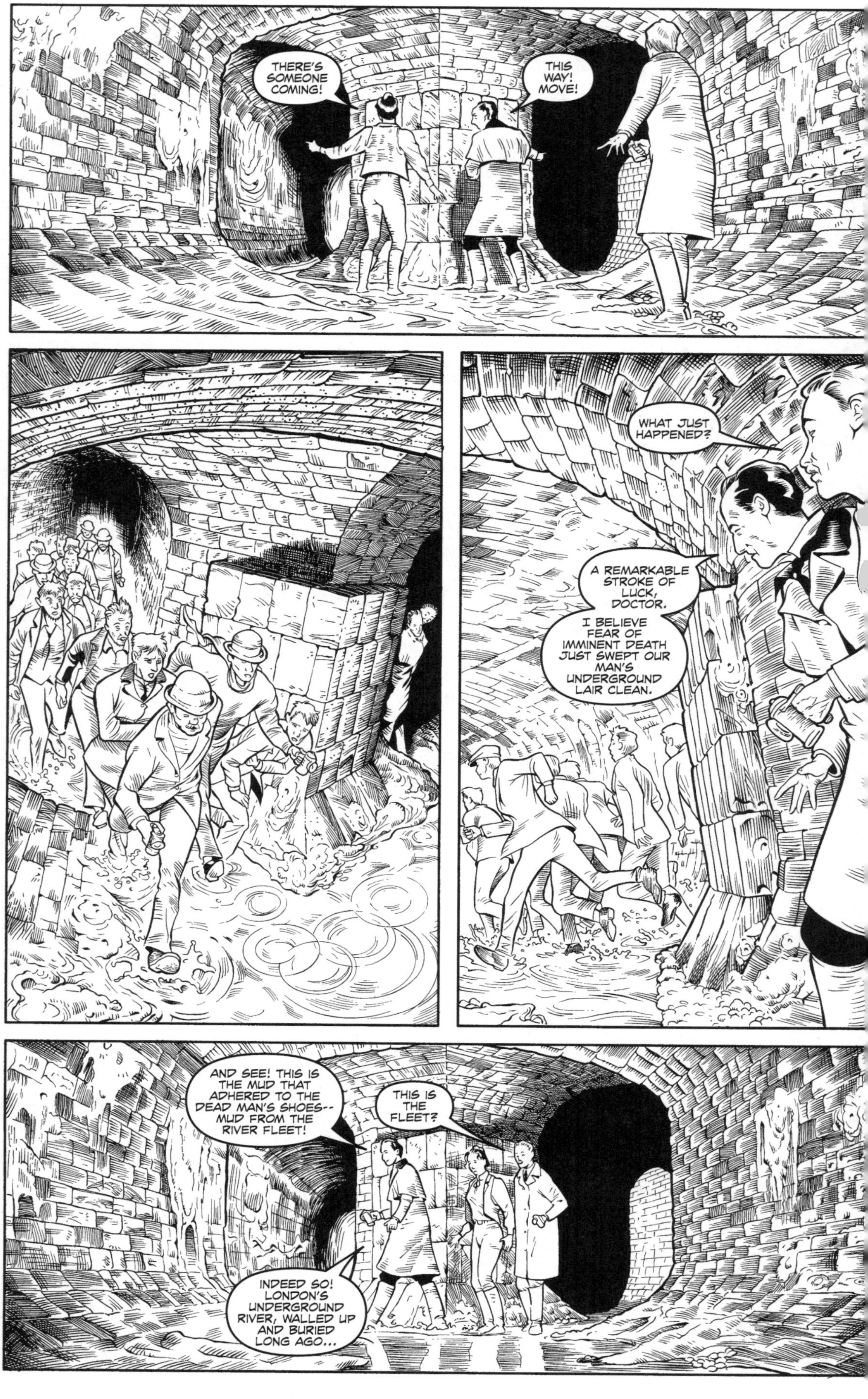
THERE'S SOMEONE COMING!
THIS WAY! MOVE!
WHAT JUST HAPPENED?
A REMARKABLE STROKE OF LUCK, DOCTOR.
I BELIEVE FEAR OF IMMINENT DEATH JUST SWEPT OUR MAN'S UNDERGROUND LAIR CLEAN.
AND SEE! THIS IS THE MUD THAT ADHERED TO THE DEAD MAN'S SHOES-- MUD FROM THE RIVER FLEET!
THIS IS THE FLEET?
INDEED SO! LONDON'S UNDERGROUND RIVER, WALLED UP AND BURIED LONG AGO...

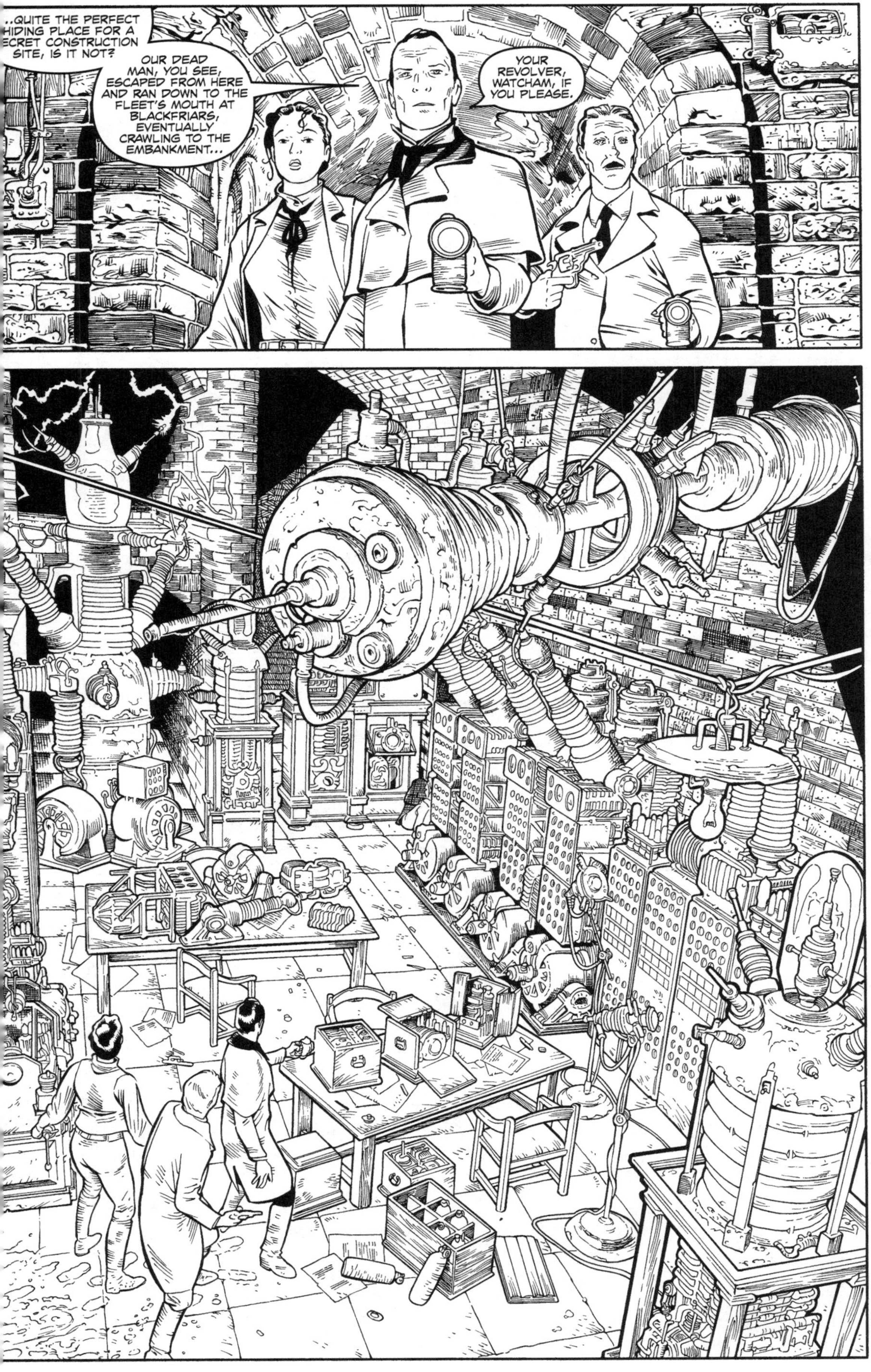
...QUITE THE PERFECT HIDING PLACE FOR A SECRET CONSTRUCTION SITE, IS IT NOT?
OUR DEAD MAN, YOU SEE, ESCAPED FROM HERE AND RAN DOWN TO THE FLEET'S MOUTH AT BLACKFRIARS, EVENTUALLY CRAWLING TO THE EMBANKMENT...
YOUR REVOLVER, WATCHAM, IF YOU PLEASE.

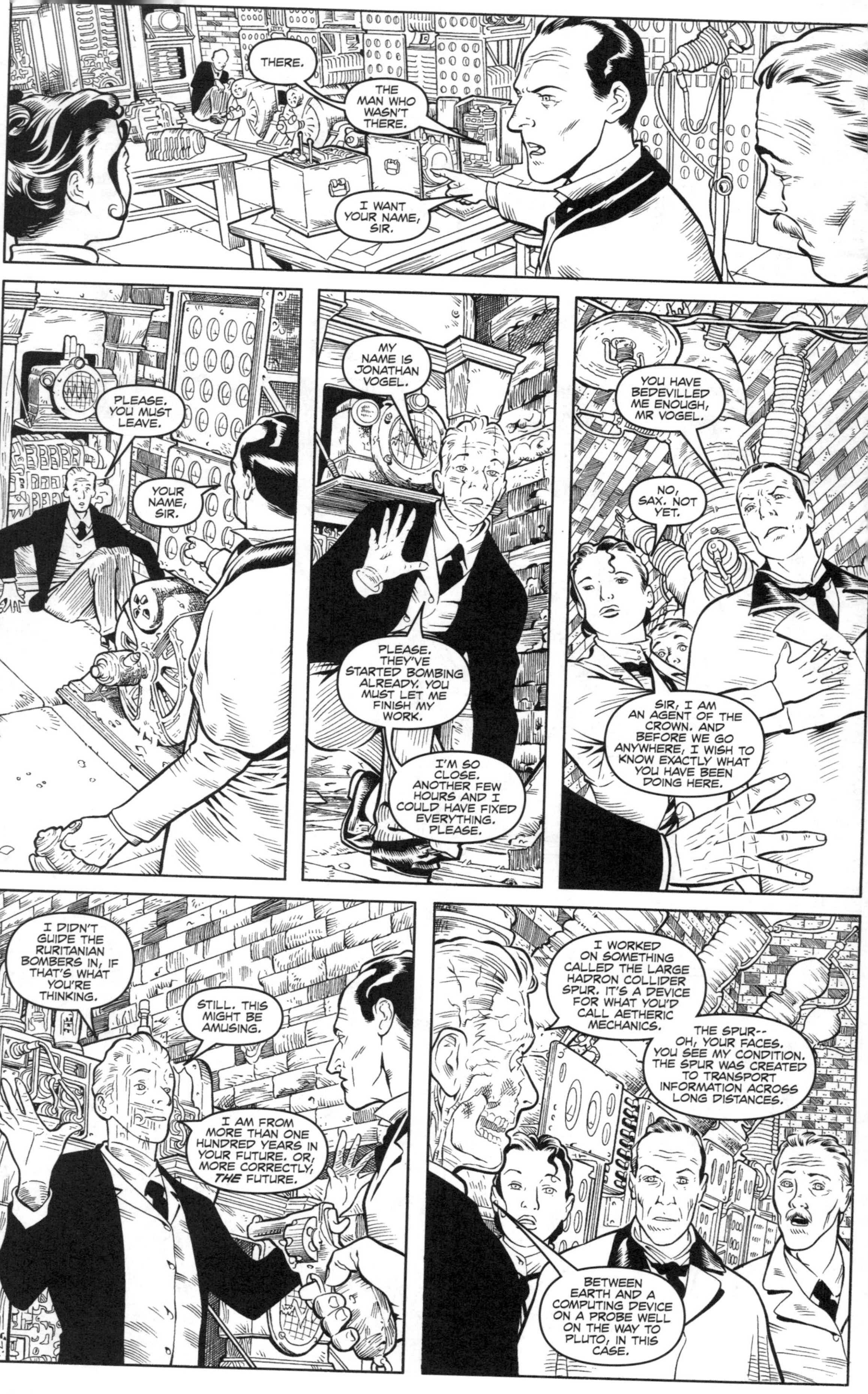
THERE.
THE MAN WHO WASN'T THERE.
I WANT YOUR NAME, SIR.
PLEASE. YOU MUST LEAVE.
YOUR NAME, SIR.
MY NAME IS JONATHAN VOGEL.
PLEASE. THEY'VE STARTED BOMBING ALREADY. YOU MUST LET ME FINISH MY WORK.
I'M SO CLOSE. ANOTHER FEW HOURS AND I COULD HAVE FIXED EVERYTHING. PLEASE.
YOU HAVE BEDEVILLED ME ENOUGH, MR VOGEL.
NO, SAX. NOT YET.
SIR, I AM AN AGENT OF THE CROWN. AND BEFORE WE GO ANYWHERE, I WISH TO KNOW EXACTLY WHAT YOU HAVE BEEN DOING HERE.
I DIDN'T GUIDE THE RURITANIAN BOMBERS IN, IF THAT'S WHAT YOU'RE THINKING.
STILL. THIS MIGHT BE AMUSING.
I AM FROM MORE THAN ONE HUNDRED YEARS IN YOUR FUTURE. OR, MORE CORRECTLY, *THE* FUTURE.
I WORKED ON SOMETHING CALLED THE LARGE HADRON COLLIDER SPUR. IT'S A DEVICE FOR WHAT YOU'D CALL AETHERIC MECHANICS.
THE SPUR-- OH, YOUR FACES. YOU SEE MY CONDITION. THE SPUR WAS CREATED TO TRANSPORT INFORMATION ACROSS LONG DISTANCES.
BETWEEN EARTH AND A COMPUTING DEVICE ON A PROBE WELL ON THE WAY TO PLUTO, IN THIS CASE.

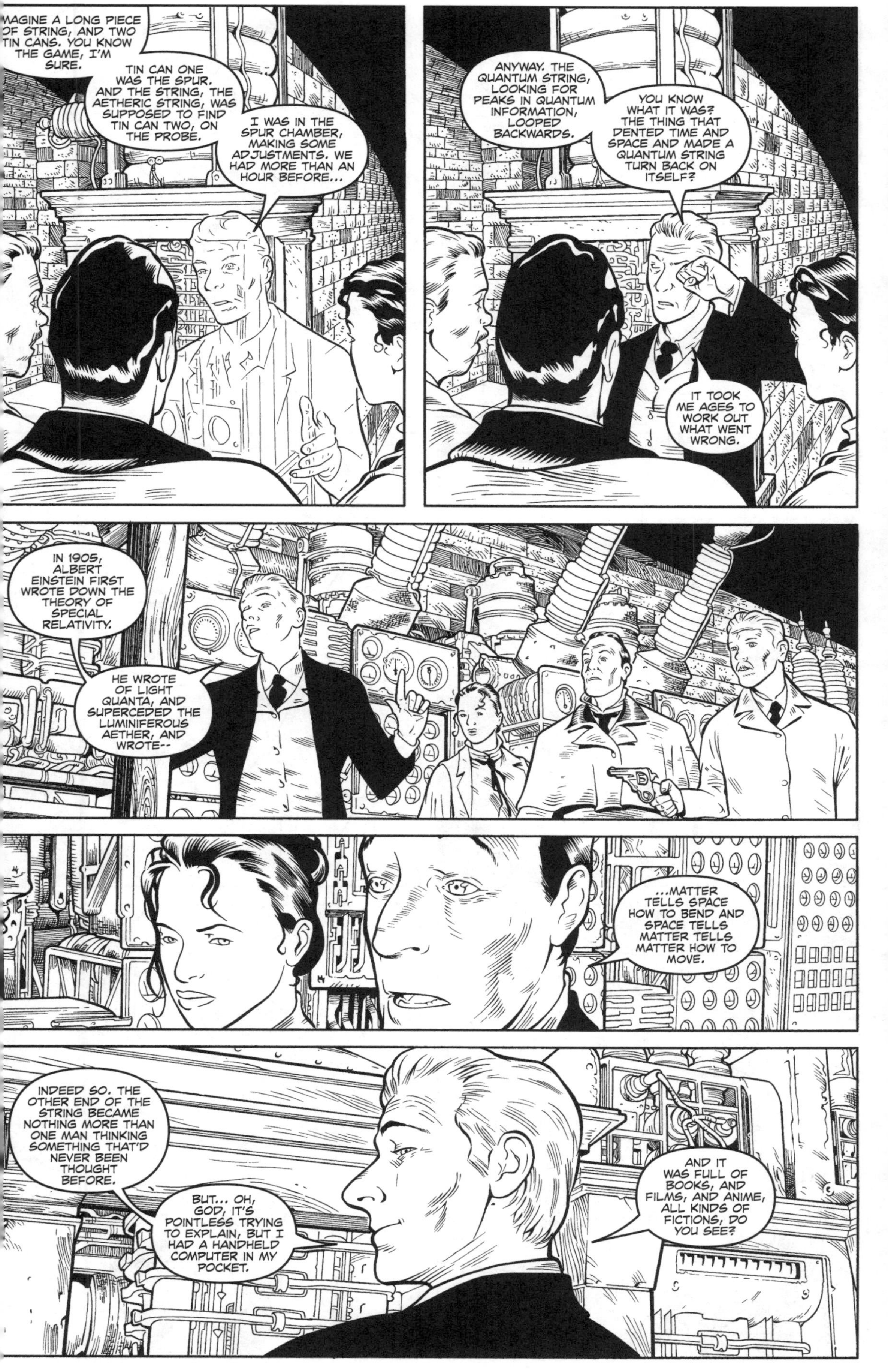
MAGINE A LONG PIECE OF STRING, AND TWO TIN CANS. YOU KNOW THE GAME, I'M SURE.
TIN CAN ONE WAS THE SPUR. AND THE STRING, THE AETHERIC STRING, WAS SUPPOSED TO FIND TIN CAN TWO, ON THE PROBE.
I WAS IN THE SPUR CHAMBER, MAKING SOME ADJUSTMENTS. WE HAD MORE THAN AN HOUR BEFORE...
ANYWAY. THE QUANTUM STRING, LOOKING FOR PEAKS IN QUANTUM INFORMATION, LOOPED BACKWARDS.
YOU KNOW WHAT IT WAS? THE THING THAT DENTED TIME AND SPACE AND MADE A QUANTUM STRING TURN BACK ON ITSELF?
IT TOOK ME AGES TO WORK OUT WHAT WENT WRONG.
IN 1905, ALBERT EINSTEIN FIRST WROTE DOWN THE THEORY OF SPECIAL RELATIVITY.
HE WROTE OF LIGHT QUANTA, AND SUPERCEDED THE LUMINIFEROUS AETHER, AND WROTE--
...MATTER TELLS SPACE HOW TO BEND AND SPACE TELLS MATTER TELLS MATTER HOW TO MOVE.
INDEED SO. THE OTHER END OF THE STRING BECAME NOTHING MORE THAN ONE MAN THINKING SOMETHING THAT'D NEVER BEEN THOUGHT BEFORE.
BUT... OH, GOD, IT'S POINTLESS TRYING TO EXPLAIN, BUT I HAD A HANDHELD COMPUTER IN MY POCKET.
AND IT WAS FULL OF BOOKS, AND FILMS, AND ANIME, ALL KINDS OF FICTIONS, DO YOU SEE?

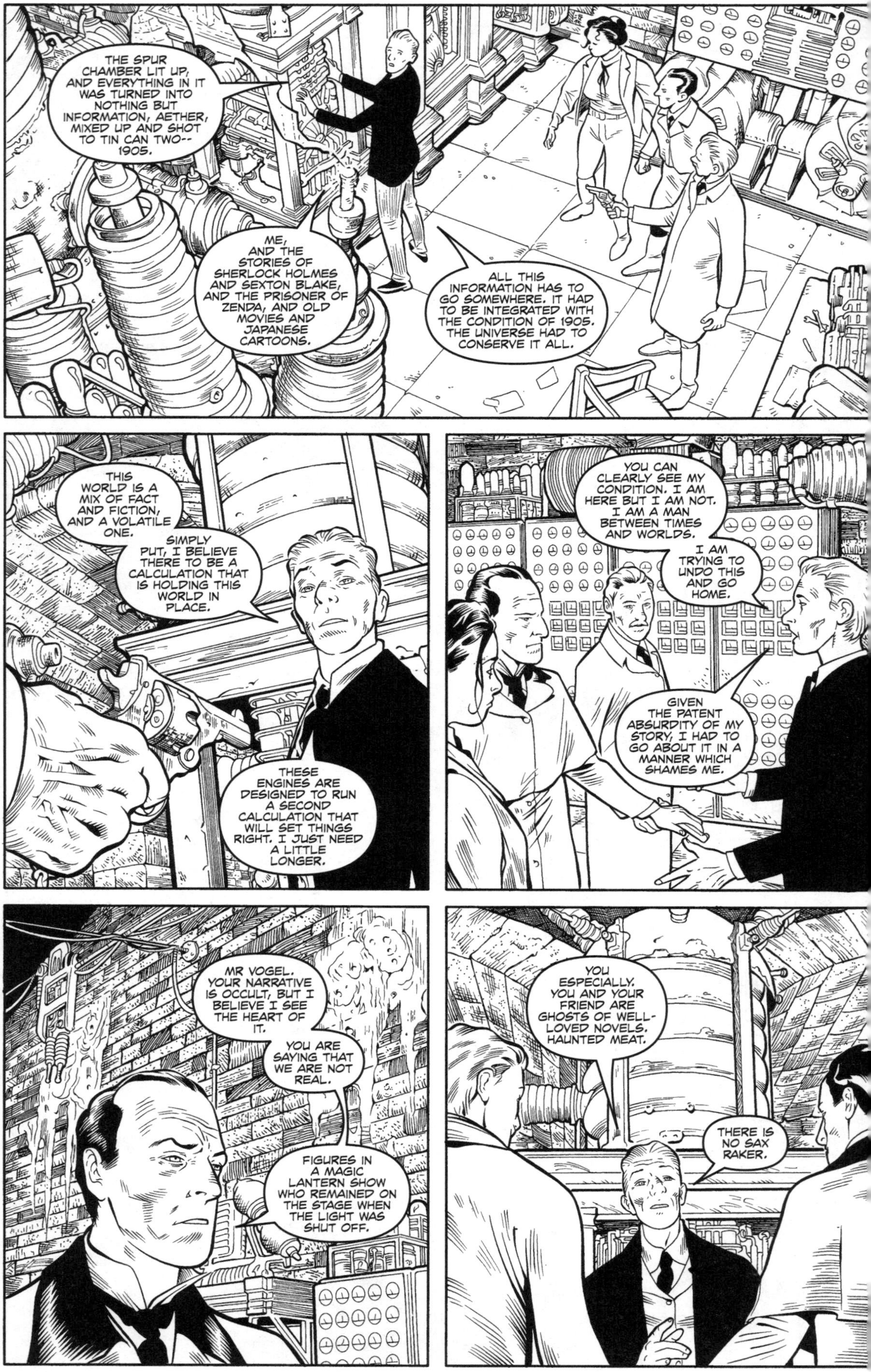

THE SPUR CHAMBER LIT UP, AND EVERYTHING IN IT WAS TURNED INTO NOTHING BUT INFORMATION, AETHER, MIXED UP AND SHOT TO TIN CAN TWO--1905.
ME, AND THE STORIES OF SHERLOCK HOLMES AND SEXTON BLAKE, AND THE PRISONER OF ZENDA, AND OLD MOVIES AND JAPANESE CARTOONS.
ALL THIS INFORMATION HAS TO GO SOMEWHERE. IT HAD TO BE INTEGRATED WITH THE CONDITION OF 1905. THE UNIVERSE HAD TO CONSERVE IT ALL.
THIS WORLD IS A MIX OF FACT AND FICTION, AND A VOLATILE ONE.
SIMPLY PUT, I BELIEVE THERE TO BE A CALCULATION THAT IS HOLDING THIS WORLD IN PLACE.
THESE ENGINES ARE DESIGNED TO RUN A SECOND CALCULATION THAT WILL SET THINGS RIGHT. I JUST NEED A LITTLE LONGER.
YOU CAN CLEARLY SEE MY CONDITION. I AM HERE BUT I AM NOT. I AM A MAN BETWEEN TIMES AND WORLDS.
I AM TRYING TO UNDO THIS AND GO HOME.
GIVEN THE PATENT ABSURDITY OF MY STORY, I HAD TO GO ABOUT IT IN A MANNER WHICH SHAMES ME.
MR VOGEL. YOUR NARRATIVE IS OCCULT, BUT I BELIEVE I SEE THE HEART OF IT.
YOU ARE SAYING THAT WE ARE NOT REAL.
FIGURES IN A MAGIC LANTERN SHOW WHO REMAINED ON THE STAGE WHEN THE LIGHT WAS SHUT OFF.
YOU ESPECIALLY. YOU AND YOUR FRIEND ARE GHOSTS OF WELL-LOVED NOVELS. HAUNTED MEAT.
THERE IS NO SAX RAKER.

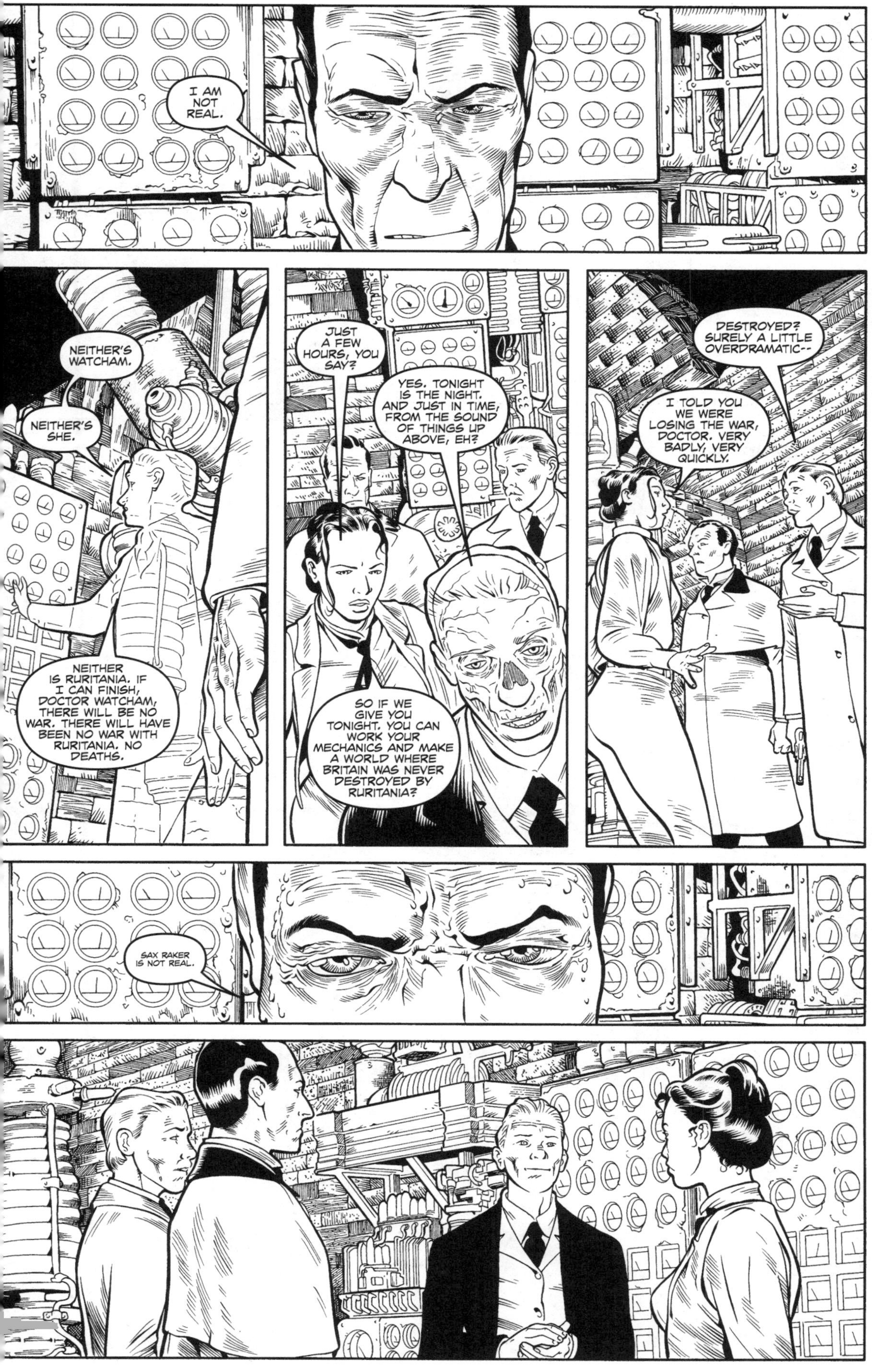
I AM NOT REAL.
NEITHER'S WATCHAM.
NEITHER'S SHE.
NEITHER IS RURITANIA. IF I CAN FINISH, DOCTOR WATCHAM, THERE WILL BE NO WAR. THERE WILL HAVE BEEN NO WAR WITH RURITANIA. NO DEATHS.
JUST A FEW HOURS, YOU SAY?
YES. TONIGHT IS THE NIGHT. AND JUST IN TIME, FROM THE SOUND OF THINGS UP ABOVE, EH?
SO IF WE GIVE YOU TONIGHT, YOU CAN WORK YOUR MECHANICS AND MAKE A WORLD WHERE BRITAIN WAS NEVER DESTROYED BY RURITANIA?
DESTROYED? SURELY A LITTLE OVERDRAMATIC--
I TOLD YOU WE WERE LOSING THE WAR, DOCTOR. VERY BADLY, VERY QUICKLY.
SAX RAKER IS NOT REAL.

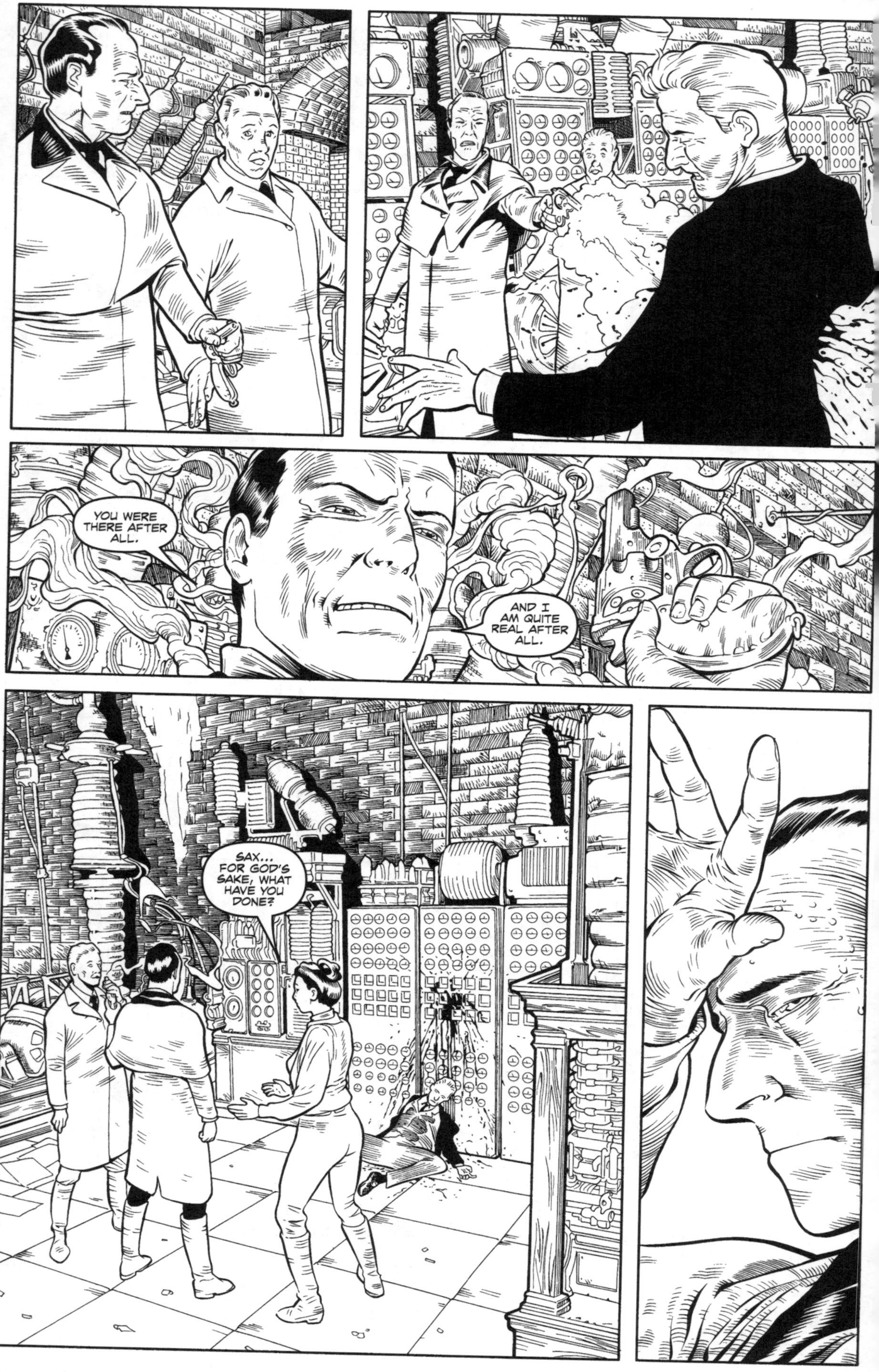
YOU WERE THERE AFTER ALL.
AND I AM QUITE REAL AFTER ALL.
SAX... FOR GOD'S SAKE, WHAT HAVE YOU DONE?

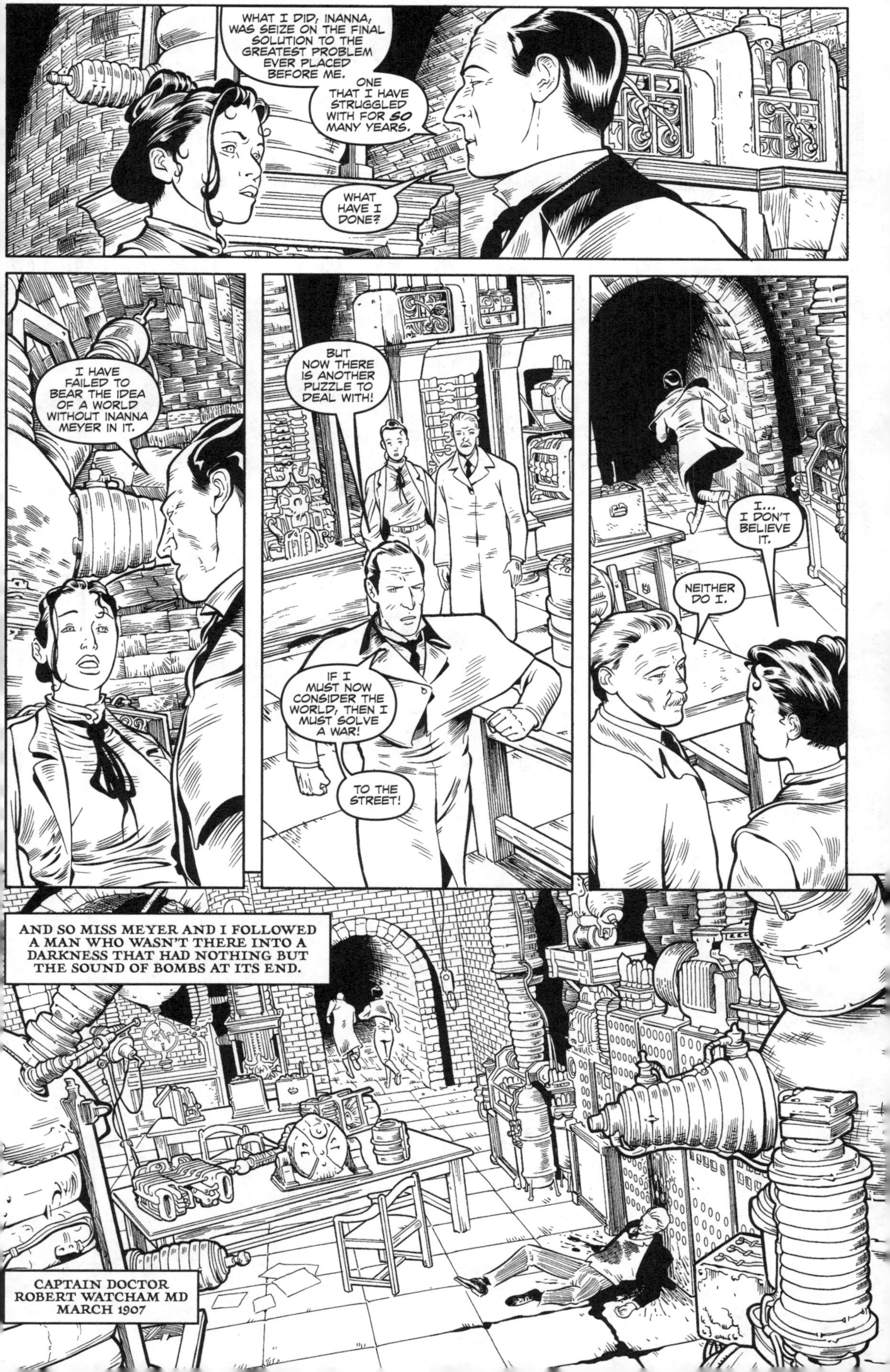
WHAT I DID, INANNA, WAS SEIZE ON THE FINAL SOLUTION TO THE GREATEST PROBLEM EVER PLACED BEFORE ME.
ONE THAT I HAVE STRUGGLED WITH FOR SO MANY YEARS.
WHAT HAVE I DONE?
I HAVE FAILED TO BEAR THE IDEA OF A WORLD WITHOUT INANNA MEYER IN IT.
BUT NOW THERE IS ANOTHER PUZZLE TO DEAL WITH!
IF I MUST NOW CONSIDER THE WORLD, THEN I MUST SOLVE A WAR!
TO THE STREET!
I... I DON'T BELIEVE IT.
NEITHER DO I.
AND SO MISS MEYER AND I FOLLOWED A MAN WHO WASN'T THERE INTO A DARKNESS THAT HAD NOTHING BUT THE SOUND OF BOMBS AT ITS END.
CAPTAIN DOCTOR ROBERT WATCHAM MD MARCH 1907

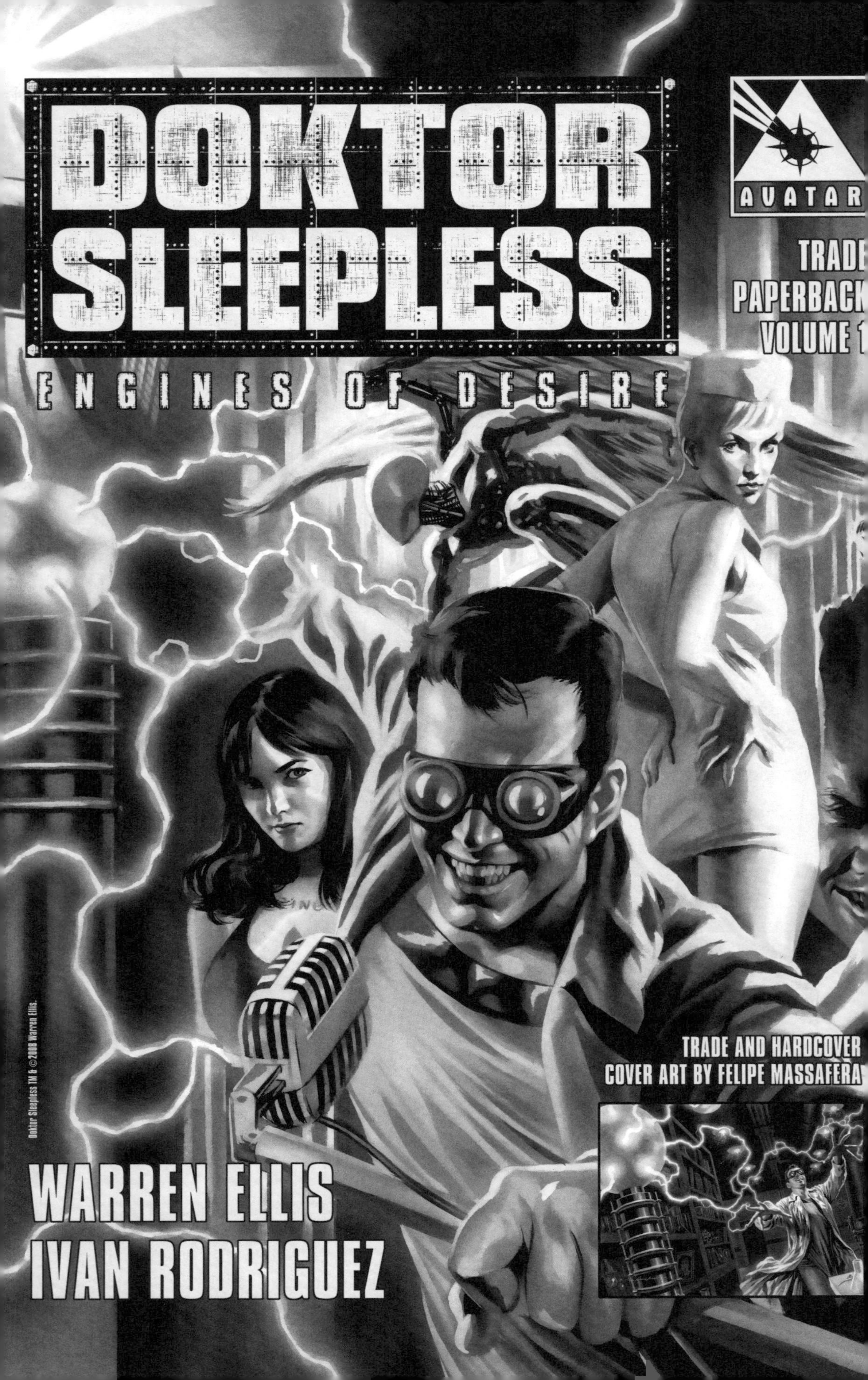
DOKTOR SLEEPLESS
ENGINES OF DESIRE
AVATAR
TRADE PAPERBACK VOLUME 1
TRADE AND HARDCOVER COVER ART BY FELIPE MASSAFERA
WARREN ELLIS
IVAN RODRIGUEZ
Doktor Sleepless TM & © 2008 Warren Ellis.

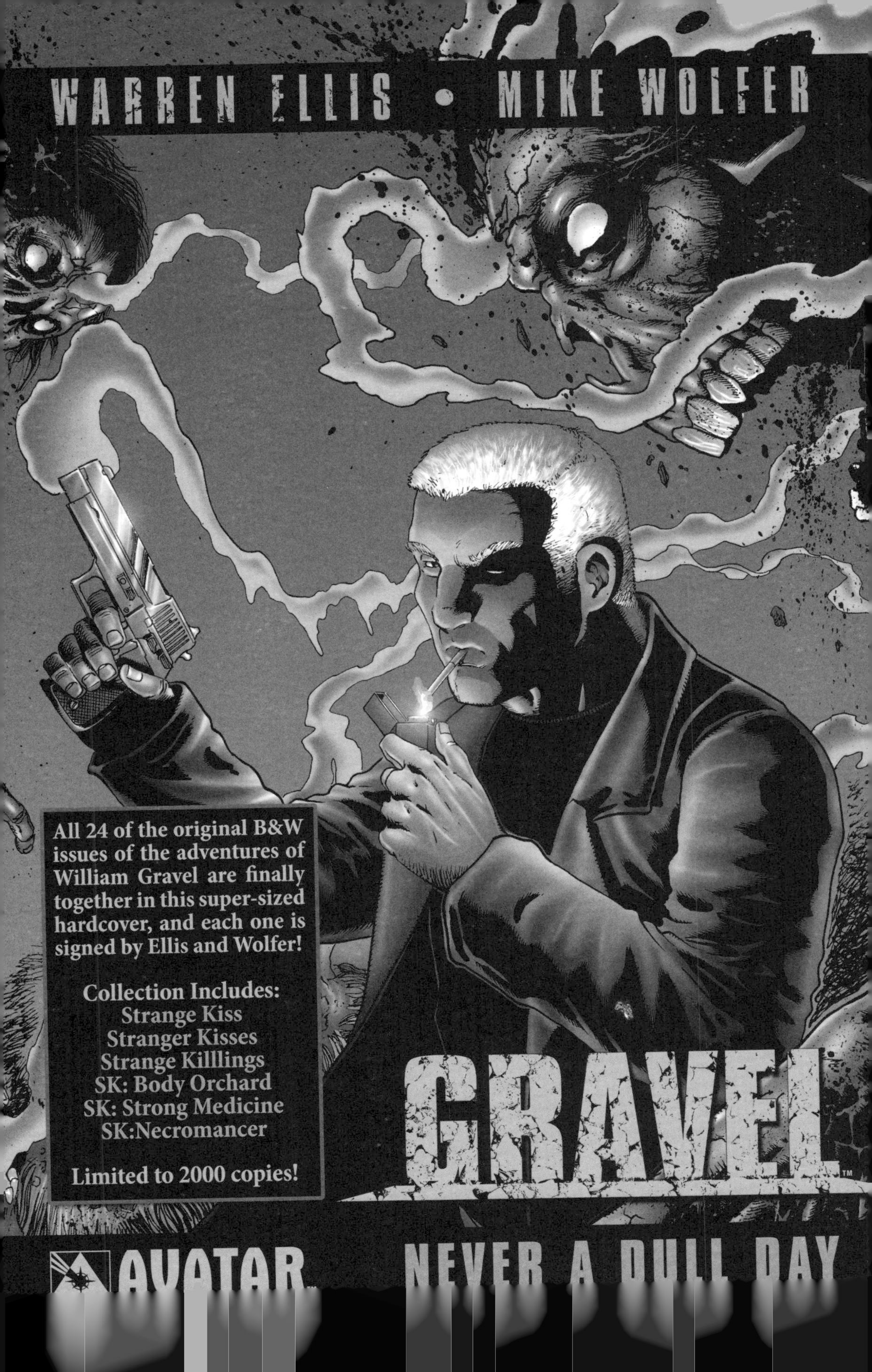
WARREN ELLIS • MIKE WOLFER
All 24 of the original B&W issues of the adventures of William Gravel are finally together in this super-sized hardcover, and each one is signed by Ellis and Wolfer!
Collection Includes:
Strange Kiss
Stranger Kisses
Strange Killlings
SK: Body Orchard
SK: Strong Medicine
SK:Necromancer
Limited to 2000 copies!
GRAVEL™
AVATAR
NEVER A DULL DAY